Cadaver 4

Copyright © 2023 Nick Clausen

Edited by Diana Cox

Created with Atticus

The author asserts his moral rights to this work.

Please respect the hard work of the author.

Any resemblance to real persons, living or undead, is purely coincidental.

1

It should be easy.

Just let go, land, and climb to safety. He even has the female cop ready to help him out. She'll grab him if he goes astray. At least if he's within reach.

But Aksel is exhausted. His muscles are worn, making his movements stiff, his reactions delayed.

Add to that the fact that his life is literally at stake, and it's not easy at all.

And he messes up.

He feels it the split-second his hands let go of the wire. His grip is way too crampy, and his fingers are reluctant to open. This means he doesn't drop straight down, but instead tilts backwards—which is hands down the worst that could have happened, because that means he'll land on his ass or worse, his back.

And as soon as he begins falling, it's too late. There's no way he's correcting his balance and bringing his legs back under his body. He's completely at the mercy of gravity and rotational momentum.

The cop sees it and cries out something Aksel doesn't register. The only thing he's aware of at that moment is a starkly vivid image that flashes into his mind, clearing out everything else.

Jakob.

Lying there.

Fallen. Broken. Dead.

And now, Aksel is falling too. He will break. He will die.

"No!"

The word thrusts itself up from his lower belly and out of his mouth in a hoarse, animallike roar.

At the same time, Aksel swings his flailing arms to the left, his legs to the right, twisting his spine in order to turn over. It's like he's seen cats do, except Aksel has no tail to help him along, and he's much less graceful.

Yet he manages to flip his upper body around just enough that he can catch the cop's hands. His lower body is still facing at a ninety-degree angle from the rest of him, and as his hip connects painfully with the roof of the car, his legs slam down on top of the head of the nearest zombie. It collapses with a groan, as Aksel begins kicking wildly, and the others immediately grab for him. The cop yanks him hard, and Aksel feels several sets of fingers scrape down over his shins, ankles, and feet, some of them very close to grabbing hold. But then he's out of reach, clutching the cop in an awkward embrace.

She pulls Aksel along as she ducks back into the car, and he dives headfirst after her.

And then he's inside. Landing clumsily over the middle console, he almost knocks his chin against the handbrake. Flopping sideways, he turns right-side-up, and finds himself sitting in the passenger seat, blinking.

"Christ, that was close," the cop sighs, staring at him from the driver's seat. "You okay?"

Aksel swallows and nods. "I think so."

"Quite a move you did," she says, sounding almost impressed. "I was sure you were going off the side, but then you ..." She flips over her hands, illustrating Aksel's aerial gymnastics.

"Yeah, I know," he mutters. "It was pure reflex."

"Please," Belinda says from the back, her head appearing between the seats. "I'm glad you made it, Axe. But my daughter is still down there …"

As though prompted by her mother, Rosa's voice comes from below: "Are you guys all okay?"

"We're fine, honey! Don't worry, we'll get you out of there …" Looking at Aksel, she raises her eyebrows in an expression somewhere between a plea and a question.

Aksel blinks. A few seconds ago, he narrowly dodged death—again—and he can't recall the plan. Then his hand goes to his pocket and fishes out the keychain. "All right," he mutters, clearing his throat. "Listen up, Rosa. I have this strong magnet on a string. I'll drop it from the window and lower it to the ground. You need to attach the key to the magnet so that I can pull it back in. That make sense?"

"Sure," Rosa says after only a brief pause. "But what about me?"

"Yeah," Belinda says, frowning. "How will that save my daughter?"

"Once we can get the car started, we'll drive off slowly," Aksel says. Then, addressing the floor: "Rosa, you'll have to cling on to the underside as we—"

"No way," Belinda says immediately. "That's way too dangerous. What if she's crushed? What if she can't hold on?"

"I know it's risky," Aksel says, lowering his voice. "But it's the best I've got. And I do think it can actually work."

He looks at the cop for her opinion. She seems to be lost in thought, but she comes back to as she senses both him and Belinda turning their attention on her. "I'm not sure it'll work," she says in an oddly emotionless tone. "But I can't think of anything better."

Aksel surveys her face for a moment. Something's clearly weighing heavily on her mind. She's not at all determined like she was before. In fact, she seems to have lost interest in dealing with the situation.

Aksel recalls her talking on the phone while he and Belinda were still inside the building. Whatever that call was about, it must have been something awful, because it seriously damaged her will to survive.

Belinda squeezes her lips together. Then, looking down: "Rosa, honey? Did you hear the plan?"

"Sure."

"Is there anything you can grab hold of?"

"I ... I think so. There's this pipe-thing, and I can get my arms around it. I'm not sure how long I can keep myself suspended, though."

"That's probably the exhaust pipe," Aksel chimes in. "That should hold just fine. It'll turn hot eventually, but that's not something we need to worry about, because we probably won't have to drive more than a few hundred yards or so. It's just until we've ditched the dead folks, and I'll jump out and pull her inside. Listen, Rosa, are you still wearing both shoes?"

"Yes."

"Then place your feet on the ground and only lift your upper body. Never mind it'll ruin your shoes; it'll give you a much better chance of holding on. And make sure your head is facing the front end of the car."

"Okay. I got it."

The girl sounds, if not outright scared, then at least anxious. But also surprisingly determined. As though she's focusing on the task at hand instead of being scared. Which is rather astounding, considering the circumstances and her slim chances of survival, which even she must be aware of.

Damnit, I really like her, Aksel thinks. *If anything happens to her, I'll never forgive myself.*

He's very aware that he's already emotionally come to view Rosa as a sibling, and he's not surprised at all to find that he feels just as protective of her as he did of Jakob. It's almost like losing his brother has made his mind aim his love at the girl instead. As though it still had a strong need to be the older brother, the leader, the guardian of someone.

"Can we please get moving?" Belinda says, glancing out at the dead people. The windows by now are smeared in a mixture of blood and saliva, turning everyone outside to figures moving in a bright red haze.

"Right," Aksel says, opening the ball and pulling out the string. "Ready, Rosa? I'll lower the magnet from the passenger side window now."

"I'm ready," Rosa confirms.

It's only as he goes to roll down the window that he realizes with a sinking feeling that there's a glaring hole in his plan.

He's used to driving his dad's truck, which is a lot older. It has mechanical crank handles—something no newer vehicle still comes with. The MPV only has a button. And, since the engine is shut off, it doesn't work.

"Shit," Aksel mutters.

"What's wrong?" Belinda says, sounding alarmed right away.

"I can't open the window," he says. "I'll have to smash it. Maybe if I can just punch a hole in the upper corner ..."

"That won't work," the cop says evenly. "It'll shatter. Modern car windows do that."

Aksel leans back and lets out a hard breath through his nose. "Goddamnit! So close ..."

"Are you serious?" Belinda asks, raising her voice.

"I'm sorry," Aksel mutters. "I forgot the windows couldn't be—"

"No, because you didn't think this through, did you?" she cuts him off. "You just wanted to go climbing on that stupid wire like an action hero, didn't you?"

"Listen," Aksel says, rubbing his forehead. "We can probably figure this out. We just need to—"

"Need to what?" Belinda almost shouts. "To think? Well, that's a little too late! Should have done that before we ended up here. Now we'll all die, and there's nothing we can—"

"We're not dying," Aksel growls. "Stop with the fucking disaster talk, will you? It's not helping."

"Well, you're not helping, either!" Belinda shouts in his ear.

Aksel turns in his seat to glare at her. "Not helping? If not for me, we'd all still be inside that fucking building!"

"Yes, and that would have been better!" Belinda shouts, fake-laughing, even though she sounds like she's close to tears. "Can't you see, we're trapped like rats here? In there, we at least had options! That stupid plan with the magnet was never gonna work!"

"You think of something, then," Aksel shouts. "Since you're such a fucking expert!"

"I trusted you! You told me this was the only way!"

"The only way *I could think of*," Aksel corrects her, still shouting. "I was open to other suggestions every step of the way. It's your daughter down there, and I haven't heard you come up with a single useful suggestion. All you do is panic and whine!"

Belinda's eyes turn from fiery to all-out rage. "You piece of shit!" She lunges at him, obviously intending to claw at his face, and Aksel just manages to catch her wrists before she can do so. Belinda screams obscenities at Aksel while still trying to get at him. Aksel tries to fend her off, but it's like pacifying a furious cat. The cop makes a half-hearted attempt to separate them, like a jaded boxing referee. Belinda pries her hand free and begins taking swings at Aksel, when—

Suddenly, she stops dead. Her expression goes blank. She's staring at something behind Aksel.

He turns his head and sees the window rolling down, apparently on its own accord. Before it's halfway open, the nearest zombie—a woman—sticks her arms in and grabs at Aksel. He yelps and jumps backwards, landing halfway on top of the cop. Belinda begins screaming. Aksel kicks at the woman, who's about to climb through the opening, when the window suddenly stops, then rolls back up. Aksel's shoe connects with the woman's head, pushing it back out, allowing the window to roll almost all the way up, pinning both her arms. She snarls and grabs for them, but she can't reach. Two other dead people notice the opportunity and try to squeeze their hands through the narrow opening.

Aksel is afraid the joined force will be enough to push the window down, but it holds.

"What the hell?" he cries out, climbing off the cop's lap. "Who did that?"

"It was me."

Rosa's voice makes them all look down.

"There's a button on the key, showing a window. I can control it from down here."

"Jesus Christ," Aksel breathes, looking from Belinda to the cop, smiling. "You could have warned us before testing it ..."

"I tried to," Rosa says matter of factly. "You were busy fighting."

The way she says it, it's suddenly like the ages have been reversed. As though Aksel and Belinda are the kids and Rosa the only responsible adult.

Aksel can tell Belinda feels it too, because she averts his eyes and blushes. "Sorry," she mutters—apparently addressing both him and her daughter. Then, a little louder: "Just don't press the button again, okay, honey?"

"I won't."

The sounds from the zombies are significantly louder now that the window is open. Aksel doesn't mind. Now they have what they need: a way to get the magnet out and down to the ground.

2

Kristoffer only meant to fire once, but he squeezes the trigger so hard, the nail gun goes off three or four times in rapid succession.

... *slam-hiss-slam-hiss-slam-hiss* ...

Ragnar comes running forward.

The soldier screams out, as he finally registers the pain, and Kristoffer feels the pressure from the blade against his neck increase. He instinctively leans away and grabs the soldier's wrist with his left hand, pushing it back.

He needn't have bothered, though.

The soldier wasn't trying to cut him, he was simply falling down. Still screaming, he collapses to the side, clutching his leg. Ragnar reaches them and yanks Kristoffer back, even though he's in no real danger. The soldier is so preoccupied with his leg, he doesn't even seem to register them.

"You shot me!" he cries out. "You fucking shot me, you asshole!"

"Great job," Ragnar says, letting out a hard breath. "Great job, Kris."

Kristoffer feels dizzy. His fingers go the place on his neck where the blade just was. He can't feel any cuts. He checks his fingertips. No blood, either.

"You shot me in the leg!" the soldiers wails. "It hurts so bad!"

"It's just a fucking nail," Ragnar grunts, going back to pick up his rifle.

"A *nail*?" the soldier exclaims, looking up at Kristoffer with pain and disbelief painted on his face.

"Yes, a nail," Ragnar says, returning with the rifle. "Any carpenter with a shred of self-respect has tried accidentally putting one in themselves. So stop bawling like a baby."

"But ... but *how*?" The soldier looks at the nail gun still in Kristoffer's hand. "Where the hell did you get *that* from?"

"I had it all along," Kristoffer hears himself mutter in a tone that's almost apologetic.

Ragnar loads the rifle, and, waving at Kristoffer, mutters: "Maybe step back a bit, Kris. And cover your ears."

"Wait, what are you ...?" Kristoffer asks, when the soldier cuts him off.

"No! No, no, no, wait, wait, wait! Don't do it, man! Come on! Please! Please don't!"

Ragnar ignores the pleading completely. He raises the rifle to his shoulder, closes one eye, takes careful aim at the guy, and—

"*Stop!*" Kristoffer shouts, grabbing the barrel of the rifle.

Ragnar glares at him with a mixture of anger and disbelief. "Let go of my rifle, Kris." His tone is low, hostile. "And don't ever do that again ..."

"I'm only letting go if you promise not to shoot him."

Ragnar's eyebrows, which are already close knitted, dip even lower. "Why the hell would we let him live? What's it to you? He just tried to kill you!"

"I don't want any more killing," Kristoffer says firmly. He feels the muscles around his mouth quiver, but he doesn't let go of the gun. "There's been too much death. We're supposed to fight the goddamn zombies, and we're running around shooting at each other instead! What the hell's wrong with us?" He's shouting now, but he can't stop himself. It feels like several days' worth of pent-up shock and dread are suddenly spilling out of him. He's looking from Ragnar, who's still mad-dogging him, to the soldier, who's still on the ground, staring up at them with incredulity and budding hope on his face. "So the two of you better put down the fucking hatchet, or I'm out of here, and you can have fun fighting to the death!"

He stops talking, breathing heavily.

"I promise," the soldier says quickly. "No more fighting. I never wanted it in the first place, I swear. I wasn't going to hurt anyone; I was just trying to protect myself."

Kristoffer nods, then looks at Ragnar. "And you?"

Ragnar yanks the rifle from him, and for a terrible second, Kristoffer is certain he'll shoot them both. But then he slings it over his shoulder. "All right. I'll agree not to shoot this prick." He sends the soldier a menacing look. "If he tells us everything we need to know about his psycho partner ... whatshisname?"

The soldier looks from Ragnar to Kristoffer, clearly confused. "You mean Kjell? Sure, fine, I'll—" He cuts himself off with a hiss. "Damnit! It hurts like hell ..."

Ragnar sighs. "Help him get that nail out, will you? So he can stop whining and start talking." He nods towards the cave. "There's a pair of pliers in the blue tool box. That should do the trick. I'll stay out here, keep an eye out for Rambo."

Kristoffer glances over at the dead soldier. "I really don't think he'll be coming back."

Ragnar scoffs. "You're so wide-eyed, Kris. I forget sometimes how young you are."

"You don't know Kjell," the soldier says, talking through gritted teeth. "He's not your typical ... he's not a normal person. And you just shot his brother. Shit. This is bad. I'm telling you, he's coming back. And he'll probably kill all of us."

Ragnar looks at Kristoffer, raising one eyebrow. "See? I know a psycho when I meet one."

The soldier winces again, carefully touching his blood-drenched pants. "Jesus Christ! Can we please get this over with? I'm bleeding like a pig here …"

Kristoffer frowns at Ragnar. "I can't just pull the nails out of his leg with a plier! That's not how you—"

"Sure you can," Ragnar says, having turned his back and already lost interest in the conversation. He's scanning the area and checking the monitor for the motion sensors.

Kristoffer throws out his arms. "But what if they're lodged in the bone?"

Ragnar sends him a look over his shoulder, shrugging. "Then you pull harder."

3

Holding the key in his hand feels surreal.

"So far, so good," he says, looking from the cop to Belinda.

"I can't believe that worked," the cop says as she holds out her hand.

"I know," Aksel concedes. "Let's just pray it'll start."

He doesn't really want to go there in his mind, but he has briefly considered all the things that could make the car not start. Dead battery. Empty tank. Or about a thousand things wrong with the engine. He's not a car expert by a long stretch, but he knows modern vehicles like this one have all kinds of electronic components, and if one wire is broken, burned or even just wet, that could be enough for the whole system to shut down. After all, there could very well be a reason why the guy left his seemingly perfectly fine car in the middle of the parking lot.

"Of course it'll start," Aksel says, trying to sound confident as he hands her the key.

The cop takes it, slides it into the ignition and steps on the brake.

Aksel feels Belinda's hand grab his shoulder as she leans forward. It seems like an impulse she's not even aware off, because she's staring at the dashboard.

The cop turns the key halfway, and all the lights come on. Aksel notices the fuel indicator shows four out of five bars. No warning signals, except for the one telling them the handbrake is on.

"Come on," Aksel whispers, not really sure who he's addressing.

The cop turns the key all the way. Aksel feels the engine more than he hears it. It's so low-noise, he can barely make it out over the snarls and groans from the zombies. But there's a very subtle buzz in his seat, which tells him the engine turned on without so much as a huff.

"Did it start?" Belinda almost shrieks, clutching Aksel's shoulder. "Is it on?"

"It is," the cop says plainly, as though she was never nervous—or maybe she just didn't really give a damn.

"Thank God!" Belinda sighs.

"Okay, Rosa!" Aksel calls out, leaning forward. "You ready? We're gonna drive now."

A moment's pause, then the girl calls back: "Ready!"

"Hold on with all you've got, honey!" Belinda tells her. "It'll only take a minute or so, and then you'll be safe."

"I know, Mom. I'll do my best."

"And call out if you lose your grip, all right? We'll stop immediately." As she says this, Belinda sends the cop a significant look. The cop nods in return, but as she looks away, Aksel catches her eyes, and he can tell she's thinking the same as him. That stopping will be way too late. If Rosa lets go, even the fastest reaction won't be fast enough. She'll be dead meat.

"All right," Rosa confirms simply.

Once again, Aksel is impressed by the girl's attitude. She must be exhausted, freezing, terrified. She's about to undertake a very strenuous and difficult task. One little slip-up will likely mean death. And yet she sounds collected. Focused.

Wish I had half the guts of that girl. I'd have asked Frida out weeks ago. We could have had many more nights together before—

The thought of Frida sends a stab of pain through his heart, and he willfully pushes the memory back down. He'll deal with her later. Her and Jakob. For now, it needs to be all about survival.

"I'll give it a test," the cop says, pulling Aksel from his thoughts. "I'll drive a few yards, see if we can even get it moving."

Aksel understands her doubt. There are a lot of dead people out there. When he and Belinda reached the car, there were maybe thirty or so. Now, there's at least a hundred. It reminds Aksel of the crowd at a rock concert, all of them pushing to get to the front. If the car had been any lower, they wouldn't have been able to see anything. But luckily, they're seated just high enough to look over the forest of heads and hands. The road, as opposed to the parking lot, is almost empty. If they can just make it out there, they should have a clean run.

The cop puts it in Drive, releases the handbrake and steps carefully on the gas. The car doesn't move at first—at least not forward. It's swaying back and forth because of the push from the zombies. She steps a little harder, and Aksel can finally hear the engine as the MPV begins pushing back. The zombies standing squarely in front of the car are either shoved aside or forced backwards. They stagger, some of them fall over, but they don't voluntarily get out of the way. If anything, they become more eager.

The car rolls a few yards, then the cop stops it again. "How are you holding up, Rosa?" Aksel calls out.

"Fine! It's working."

"Oh, Jesus," Belinda breathes. She's still clutching Aksel's shoulder.

"That's good," says the cop, and Aksel can tell she seems a bit more awake now. As though the task at hand has momentarily called her back from whatever stupor she was in. "Take a short break, Rosa, and then we'll go for it. I'll drive maybe five yards, then turn out onto the road. Careful as we go down the slight ramp, okay?"

"Okay."

A few seconds pass.

"You ready again?" the cop calls.

"Ready!"

The cop nods, then steps on the accelerator. The car begins pushing against the zombies, then slowly gets moving again.

Plowing through the crowd in slow motion, they are able to do exactly what Aksel was hoping: parting the dead people like Moses did the Red Sea. The car sways and rocks as they keep pushing from the sides. Aksel hears bones break from arms and legs getting caught under the tires. And the woman whose arms are pinned in his window gets dragged along for the ride, stumbling sideways while still hissing and groping for Aksel.

"Rosa, honey?" Belinda calls. "You still okay?"

No answer comes.

"Rosa!?"

"It's okay, she's focusing," Aksel says. "It's not easy holding your weight up like that. Let her concentrate."

Belinda squeezes her lips together, looking like she's fighting the urge to shout for her daughter again.

"She's still there," Aksel reassures her, adding in his mind: *If not, we would have heard her scream.*

"Okay, Rosa!" the cop shouts, turning the wheel, making the car go left. "Here comes the ramp!"

No answer from below—at least not one Aksel can make out.

The MPV dips down onto the street with one front tire, then the other, then both rear tires. It sways a little more violently than it's done so far, and Aksel hears a sound he's pretty sure comes from Rosa. It's halfway between a whimper and a grunt.

"Honey?" Belinda cries out, as she obviously hears it too. "Stop!" she yells, grabbing the cop's arm. "She slipped! Stop! Go back!"

"No," Aksel says. "Keep driving!" He pries Belinda's hand free and cups it in both of his own, catching Belinda's terrified eyes. "It's all right. She'll call out if we need to stop. Okay?"

Belinda is breathing raggedly, but she manages to give a nod. She looks like she wants to puke or cry or both.

"Damnit," the cop hisses. "They're not backing off …"

Aksel looks out and sees how the crowd is following them like paparazzi stalking a celebrity. They are falling behind, but slowly. There are still a bunch of them in front of the car, and several more flanking the sides, staggering along.

"I need to speed up," the cop mutters. "Hold on, Rosa! Just a few more second now!"

The car picks up speed. And it works. The zombies can only muster what's equivalent to a brisk walk, and the car finally starts coming out of the woods. But the added speed also means that the ones in front are now getting run over instead of pushed aside, and the car bobs and sways hard as the tires rolls over the falling bodies.

"Hold on, Rosa!" Belinda screams.

Aksel looks back. Seeing most of the crowd fall behind them, he's shocked to find just how many of the dead people had surrounded them. They take up most of the street. Some of them are already losing interest in trying to keep up with the car, and are headed off in other directions, hoping to find easier prey. The front runners, however, are still trying to close the growing gap to the MPV.

"She's still there," Aksel hears himself say. "She's still hanging on."

He begins to hope they'll actually make it, when the cop exclaims: "Fuck!"

Turning around, he sees a big, bald-shaven guy latching on to the hood of the car. He seems to have used one of his fallen comrades as a springboard, and he's managed to latch on to the wipers. He's mashing his face against the windscreen, trying to bite at the cop.

She sends a gust of washer fluid up into his face, but it hardly seems to bother him. Instead she swerves the wheel gently back and forth. The zombie swings from side to side but doesn't let go.

"I'll deal with him," Aksel says. "Just keep driving."

The woman in his window is still along for the ride, though they're going so fast now, she's actually getting dragged rather than walking on her own. Aksel hits the button and rolls down the window. The woman drops with a snarl and disappears from sight. Aksel leans out the window and shouts: "Hold on, Rosa! Almost there!"

He reaches around to the front and catches the guy's ankle. Pulling hard, he manages to drag both his legs off the hood. The zombie grunts and holds on, but now that he's hanging with all his weight on one of the wipers, it can't hold, and it breaks. The guy falls off, landing hard on the concrete, rolling around several times.

Aksel pulls back inside and looks out the rear window. Almost all of the undead have given up the chase. Only half a dozen seem hell-bent on catching up with the car, but they're twenty yards away.

"Okay, we're clear!" the cop says. "Get ready, Aksel!"

"Ready!"

The cop locks the brakes, and Aksel pushes open the door, throws himself out and drops to the ground. As he looks under the car, he's afraid of what he'll see.

Worst of all would be nothing—no Rosa.

Almost as bad would be Rosa, beaten and scraped bloody from the ride.

What he does see is the girl, both arms wrapped around the exhaustion pipe, her eyes squeezed shut, her face determined. She's only wearing one shoe, and it's been almost torn to shreds but it's still on her foot.

"Rosa!" he shouts, reaching in his hand. "Come on! Go, go, go!"

The girl opens her eyes, turns her head, and is obviously surprised to see his face. She only needs half a second to react. Unwrapping her arms, she slumps to the ground. She tries to roll over, tries to crawl towards him, but her strength is failing, and all she manages is to reach out her arm.

It's enough, though.

Aksel grabs her frozen hand and yanks hard. The girl slides across asphalt. She has to turn her head sideways and exhale in order to get her head and chest out from under the car.

Belinda has opened her own door and is screaming from inside the car. She's leaning out, reaching for Rosa with both arms, and if the cop hadn't held her back, she would probably have come tumbling out.

Aksel doesn't wait for Rosa to get up on her own—she probably can't—so he simply hoists her up like a big dummy and all but throws her into the arms of her mother. He slams the door, and as he turns to jump in himself, the bald guy lunges for him. Out of pure reflex, Aksel pushes himself away from the car, and the guy bumps into the just-closed door. Aksel narrowly escapes and stumbles away. Turning, he sees the guy go for the open door, and he shouts for the cop to drive.

She doesn't need the instruction, as she already stomped the accelerator. The MPV lunges forward half a second before the bald guy can jump in. Instead, he tries to grab hold of the side of the car, only managing to stumble and fall flat on his face.

"Yes!" Aksel exclaims in triumph. "We did it!"

Then he suddenly becomes aware of the fact that even though Rosa is safe inside the car, he himself is now standing in the middle of the road, unarmed and completely exposed.

The bald guy is already getting back up, and as Aksel glances back, he sees the group of front runners coming for him fast. Other random striders are closing in from the sides as well, and within seconds, Aksel will be torn apart alive. He gets moving, dodging the bald guy like an American footballer, and sprints for the car. The cop has slowed down without stopping completely, and the door is still open.

Aksel was always a fast runner, and he catches up quickly. Throwing himself inside, he slams the door, and the cop floors it. The MPV's engine gives a willing roar, as though it's been waiting impatiently to finally get going, and they accelerate fast.

"Oh, God, oh, thank heaven, oh, my sweet baby girl ..."

Aksel turns around to see Belinda clutching Rosa. The girl is trembling uncontrollably. Her lips are blue, and her teeth are literally chattering. Her eyes are alive, though. And as they fix on Aksel, a twitch at the corner of her mouth implies that the girl tries to smile at him.

4

The operation—to Kristoffer's immense relief—turns out a lot simpler and less risky than he feared.

Only two of the nails went in, and they're sitting just inside the skin. The hard part, really, is getting the guy's pants off, since they've effectively been nailed to his leg. After they manage to do that, pulling the nails out with the pliers is very straightforward and over in a couple of seconds. They slide out with soft, wet noises, and Kristoffer drops them to the floor.

The guy grinds his teeth, hisses and slaps his other leg as though to distract himself. "Jesus, Mary and Josef, that's the most painful thing I've ever tried …"

"Then I'm sure this won't bother you too much," Kristoffer mutters, opening the first aid kit and taking out the hydrogen peroxide. He unscrews it and splashes a little on the wounds.

The soldier cries out, pulling his leg away. "What the hell, man? You're supposed to use a cotton swab and dab it gently …"

"Sorry," Kristoffer shrugs. "I'm not a doctor."

"And you never took a first aid course either, I take it?" the guy grunts, then breaks into a nervous laugh. "Look, I'm sorry … you're a good guy. I'm just fucking stressed out here … it's been a crazy couple of days, you know? And now this messed-up situation …" He runs both hands through his hair, then back down over his face, covering his eyes and sighing deeply. "I really wanted to make it to Sweden. Now I'm gonna die in a cave instead."

"You're not dying," Kristoffer assures him, placing a wide Band-Aid over the wounds. "If it becomes septic, Ragnar has all sorts of antibiotics, and I'm sure we can—"

"I'm not talking about that," the soldier says grimly. "I'm talking about Kjell. He never liked me. It was Lukas who convinced him to bring me along, because I'm the one with the contact in Sweden. Anyway, now that Lukas is dead, I'm sure Kjell will enjoy killing me just for the sport of it."

Kristoffer frowns. "No one's like that in real life."

The guy huffs. "You don't know Kjell, then."

"No, we don't," Ragnar says, suddenly standing there. "So please, fill us in."

The soldier licks his lips, looking from Kristoffer to Ragnar, seemingly uncertain where to begin. He reaches into his breast pocket and pulls out a packet of chewing gum, popping two into his mouth. Apparently, he either swallowed or dropped the gum he was already chewing sometime during the fight.

"I'm Kris by the way," Kristoffer says, helping the guy break the ice. "This is Ragnar."

"Yeah, I got that," the soldier says, smacking away at the new gum. "I'm Jan." He takes a breath. "All right, so, here's the deal. Kjell is a maniac. Like, a proper psycho. I'm positive he murdered kittens and stuff as a child. I don't think he was ever convicted of anything, but he fits the profile perfectly. I've known him for eight, nine years or something, and he'll still give me the creeps sometimes when he talks." The soldier shrugs. "He's got no empathy. He only cares about himself, and maybe his older brother. Lukas was the only family he had, and now that you killed him ..." Jan looks at Ragnar and shakes his head. "There's no way in hell he's letting that slide."

"Of course not," Ragnar says simply. "I sure wouldn't. So, what can we expect? Will he come in swinging, or is he stealthy type?"

Jan works the gum hard, his eyes darting around the cave for a few seconds. "Neither of them, I think. I mean, he can be very sneaky when he wants to. You saw how he and Lukas slipped up on you guys without a sound. It was me who tripped that alarm; Kjell would never be so careless. He's trained for shit like that. I'm just a radio operator."

"So there's no need to set up anymore trip wires," Ragnar concludes. "How do you think he'll be coming for us?"

Jan shakes his head. "I don't know. Honestly. I'm sure he'll think of some clever way. He's a great problem solver, and he's got that devious way of thinking. Like, this one time, he told me about how three guys came for him back in college. He'd provoked them or something, so they followed him to the restroom to kick his ass. He locked himself in a stall, and there was no way to get out. Still, he walked away without a scratch." Jan raises his eyebrows. "You know how he got outta there?"

Ragnar doesn't say anything, so Kristoffer clears his throat. "How did he do it?"

"He shat in his own hand, opened the door, and threw it in their faces. One of them still came for him, so he poked his eye out with the key for his scooter. He was a juvenile, so he just got transferred to another school."

"Fuck," Kristoffer mutters.

"All right," Ragnar says in a surprisingly even tone. "So he's not afraid to get his hands dirty, and he likes to be dramatic. Good to know." Then, as though the subject has been covered, he points over his shoulder and says, "I'm hungry, so I'll get the fire going. You guys can—"

"Wait," Kristoffer cuts him off as Ragnar is about to leave. "You can't go out there."

"Why not?"

"Well, he's still out there. He could be lying in wait. He might shoot you as soon as you step outside."

"Nah," Ragnar says, squeezing his lips shut while pulling down the corners of his mouth—it's something Kristoffer has noticed him doing often, and it reminds him of Robert De Niro. "He won't do that. It would be way too easy."

Kristoffer looks at Jan for confirmation.

Jan shrugs. "I don't know, but ... I think you could be right."

"Trust me," Ragnar says. "If he wanted to just shoot us, he would have come for us already. No, he's—"

Ragnar stops talking as a phone starts chiming.

Jan fumbles for the backpack. Kristoffer is surprised he's getting a signal up here, but it makes sense when he actually sees Jan pull out the phone. It's not a regular cell, but an old-school looking device with push-buttons and a narrow display. It also has a thick, foldable antenna.

"That him?" Ragnar asks as Jan just stares at the display.

The soldier blinks and looks up. "Uh-huh."

5

It's not exactly comfortable lying on the hard concrete. And she really wishes she was wearing a jacket. Now that the worst of the fear has dwindled somewhat, the cold has taken over and is keeping her in an iron grip, making it hard to move her arms and legs properly. Her nose feels like an icicle, her butt is numb, and even though she keeps blowing into her hands, her fingers are all stiff.

At first, she was terrified at the sight of the dead people trying to get to her from all sides. Their black eyes staring hungrily at her, their snapping mouths dripping with foam, their greenish hands clawing away. Once she realized they couldn't get to her no matter how badly they wanted, she was able to relax a little. The car is made in such a way that the sides, front and back are all very low, while the actual undercarriage is taller. So even though she had to push hard initially to get under the car, now that she's here, she has enough room to turn over—which she does. Having to catch the magnet and fasten the key to it seems easier while lying on her stomach.

"*Okay, Rosa,*" Aksel says from above, speaking loud enough to drown out the choir of moans and groans from the zombies. "Here it comes ... *I'm lowering it now.*"

Rosa turns her head toward where she assumes the front passenger door must be—the only thing she has to go on are the tires, as the rest of the view is blocked by dead people.

She waits, looks, holding her breath.

"*You see it?*" Aksel shouts.

"No!"

"It should be on the ground now ..."

"I don't see it anywhere."

"Hold on ... I'll pull it back up and try again ... Damnit!"

"What is it?" Mom's voice.

"The string's gotten entangled in something ... There, it came free ... Okay, take two ..."

Rosa looks, but still doesn't see the magnet.

Aksel tries a few more times without any luck.

Mom asks if he's sure this'll work.

Rosa is beginning to wonder about that, too—when suddenly, she sees something silvery. There's a very thin, almost invisible string, too.

"Stop!" she calls out, as Aksel is about to pull the magnet back up. "I see it! I see it, Aksel!"

"You do?"

"Uh-huh. But there's a woman ... she keeps covering it with her arm ... I don't know if I can get to it without her grabbing me ..."

"Be careful, honey!" Mom urges her, sounding immediately alarmed. *"Don't take any chances ..."*

"No, I won't," Rosa says, chewing her frozen lip. Her heart is beating fast. The magnet is right there, three feet away. If the zombies hadn't been there, she could simply reach out her hand and take it.

"Can you use your leg, maybe?" Aksel suggests. *"They can't easily bite through shoes."*

"No, but they can tear it off," Mom says. *"She needs something else ..."*

"There's nothing here," Rosa says, glancing around, even though she knows it's just her down here.

"Maybe there's something inside the car," the cop suggests—it's the first time Rosa hears her speak, and her voice is weirdly dreamy. *"I saw an umbrella in the back when I searched for the key."*

"Let me get it," Mom says.

Rosa waits.

"Okay, Rosa," Aksel says. "*I'm going to drop the umbrella from the window. We only get one shot. I can't pull it back up like I did with the string. You ready?*"

"Ready," Rosa confirms.

"*Here it comes ...*"

Rosa doesn't see it right away. It probably lands on top of the zombies. Then she catches sight of something red. The umbrella has made it to the ground, but it's even farther away than the magnet—and because of how the dead guy next to the woman is pushing against the car, his knee shoves the umbrella back a few more feet, placing it way outside of Rosa's reach.

"It's gone," she says with a sigh. "I can't reach it."

"*Fuck!*" Aksel says. "*All right, Rosa, give us a minute to check for anything else ...*"

A minute passes. Then another one. She can hear them talking together. She doesn't take her eyes off the magnet. It's moving a little back and forth because of the woman's movements, but it largely stays in place, right below her left armpit.

"*I have a belt*," Aksel says finally. "*That's really the only thing we've got, Rosa. You think that'll work?*"

Rosa considers. She's been staring at the magnet, but now she notices something else. The zombie on the other side of the woman—an older guy—keeps trying to edge in from the side. He's halfway behind the wheel, and that seems to bother him. He keeps moving his head sideways, as though trying to see Rosa. It gives her an idea.

"I think I'll try something else," she says. "I don't know if it'll work, but ..."

"*What is it?*" Mom asks sharply. "*Is it risky?*"

"A little, maybe. I'll take off my shirt, and I'll throw it in the face of the woman. If she can't see me, she can't grab me. If I can just blind her for two seconds, I can grab the magnet."

She expects Mom to object, but she doesn't. A moment of silence follows.

When someone does speak, it's not her mom, but Aksel. "*I don't think that's a bad idea. But maybe use your pants instead. And put your socks on your hands. That way, they'll be better protected if she scratches you by accident.*"

"All right," Rosa says. She begins pulling off her shoes, socks and pants. It's difficult because of the narrow space and her frozen hands. But she manages. The skin on her legs is already cold, but placing it against the icy concrete, it begins outright hurting. She ignores it as best she can, puts one of her socks on her right hand, and then sticks her left hand into one of her shoes. Then she takes the pants, gathers them into a bundle, and moves very slowly and carefully closer to the woman. When she's only inches out of her reach, Rosa stops. The woman gets riled up by Rosa coming closer, and she snarls and moans and claws away eagerly.

"I'll do it now," she says, hearing her own voice falter a little. She's not sure if it's fear or the cold that's making her tremble all over.

"*Please, please be careful, honey,*" Mom says, sounding on the verge of tears.

"I will," Rosa promises.

Then she takes two more breaths, and she flings the pants into the face of the woman.

She can tell right away that it works. The woman gives off an annoyed grunt and begins thrashing to get the pants off. When that doesn't work, she uses her hands—which means she's no longer reaching for Rosa.

Rosa immediately moves closer and goes for the magnet with her sock-hand. She grabs it, and just as she pulls back, the woman manages to rip the pants aside, and her black eyes fix on Rosa right away, visibly surprised to see her this close. Rosa screams out and lifts her left hand as the woman grabs for her. She catches her wrist—Rosa is thankful that Aksel made her use her pants instead of her shirt—and pulls hard. Rosa yanks her arm the other way, but the woman is too strong. Rosa screams as the woman pulls her arm to her mouth, opens wide and bites down hard right on the tip of the shoe. Rosa tugs her arm back hard again, and this time, her hand slips out of the shoe, and she's free. But she's also still within reach of the woman. Luckily, the zombie spends a couple of seconds chewing fiercely away at Rosa's shoe, and it's all she needs to pull back into the center of the car and out of reach.

She lies there for a moment, her heart pounding so hard it's making her dizzy. She can't hear anything but the woman's angry snarl as she realizes the shoe isn't edible, pushes it aside and instead resumes trying to reach Rosa.

Slowly, other sounds return, and she becomes aware that her mom is screaming for her.

"Rosa?! ... **Rosaaa**?! ... *Are you okay?* ... Oh, God! ... **Rosa**?!"

"I'm ... fine," Rosa croaks. She clears her throat, and calls out, a little louder: "I'm fine, Mom. Nothing happened to me."

"*Oh, thank heaven!*" her mom exclaims. "*Are you sure? Are you sure you're okay?*"

"I am," Rosa says, turning over her frozen hand. It's completely unscathed. Not a single scratch. Had she not worn the shoe, she would no doubt be looking at a bloody mess with missing fingers and bones sticking.

"*The magnet?*" Aksel asks. "*Did you get it?*"

Rosa realizes to her horror that she forgot all about the magnet. She turns her head to look at her sock hand. It's still clutched into a fist. The thin, transparent nylon string runs out from between her thumb and the rest of her fingers. And, as her freezing, cramped-up hand reluctantly opens, she sees the magnet lying there.

"I got it," she whispers. "I got it!"

"*Yes!*" Aksel shouts, sounding like he's watching a game on TV and his team just scoring. "*Awesome! You're such a rockstar, Rosa! Well done!*"

Rosa can't help but smile. Her cheeks are so frozen by now, they can hardly move. Her nose and eyes are running, and she's shivering badly. Even talking is hard. "I'll attach ... the key now," she says.

The key is still there, on the ground, and it clicks onto the magnet willingly.

"Okay, Axe," she calls, placing the key and the magnet on the concrete. "You can pull it up now."

For a few seconds nothing happens. Then the string slowly tightens, and the magnet begins sliding across the ground. Rosa follows it with her eyes, holding her breath. It won't be easy. The string seems like it's running close up against the car door, so hopefully nothing will block its way. But first, it needs to get past the woman. It's running right past her face. The magnet is pulled in between her groping hands, and for a moment, Rosa fears she'll grab the key and yank it off. That would be all it took to ruin their escape.

But of course, the woman has no idea what they're trying to do, and she doesn't even seem to notice the magnet. It continues closer to her face, pauses briefly next to her chin, then lifts off the ground and dangles like a hovering earring just inches from the side of her face. She moves her head, bumping against the magnet, and it sways a little. But the key stays on there. It rises farther still, and it's almost out of Rosa's sight, when it gets entangled in the woman's hair.

"*Shit*," Aksel says. "*No, no, no. It's stuck on something.*"

"It's her ... hair," Rosa tells him. "Try ... jiggling it ..."

The magnet moves up and down. Carefully at first, then a little more. The key turns a little as strands of the woman's hair comes between it and the magnet, and for a terrifying moment, Rosa is sure it'll drop.

Then the woman makes another move with her head, whipping her hair to the side, and it frees the magnet right up. It rises up, bringing the key along, disappearing from sight.

"*Okay*," Aksel says. "*Okay, I think it's coming ... I think it—*" He cuts himself off with a gasp. A moment of silence. Then he shouts: "*I got it! I fucking **got it**!*"

6

"Should I answer?"

The satellite phone keeps ringing.

Both Jan and Kristoffer look at Ragnar.

"Of course you should answer," he says. "Talk to him. Tell him you shot me."

Jan frowns. "What? Why?"

Ragnar shrugs. "Because that's probably the only thing that'll deter him from coming back. But only if you make him believe I'm really dead."

Jan starts chewing away fast at his gum, as though it's a stress ball for his teeth. "I'm not sure I can sell it. He'll probably see right through it."

Ragnar crosses his arms, as though saying: "Go ahead, give it a try."

Jan glances briefly at Kristoffer, like he's looking for reassurance. Then he answers the call and places the phone to his ear. "Kjell? That you?"

Kris can't help but lean in a little closer to listen.

"*Hey, Jan,*" Kjell's voice comes over the satellite phone. "*Tell you the truth, I thought it'd be that old guy answering my call.*"

"No, no," Jan says, shaking his head as though Kjell could see him. "I killed him. He's dead." He widens his eyes and looks up at Ragnar, holding his breath.

After a pause, Kjell asks: "*Really?*"

"Yeah, man. I checked his pulse to make sure. Dead as a doornail."

"But you didn't even have a gun."

It sounds more like a statement than a question.

"I picked up one in the cave," Jan says right away, obviously ready for it. "The guy had a small arsenal. It was easy, really. I just hunkered down and waited for him to come back. Shot him right in the chest when he stepped inside."

Careful, Kristoffer thinks. *You're selling it too hard.*

Apparently, Kjell picks up on it too, because he repeats: "*In the chest, huh?*"

"Yeah. Blew his goddamn heart out for what he did. Look, man, I'm really sorry about Lukas."

"*Yeah, me too,*" Kjell says, his voice changing.

Jan seems uncertain about what to say. "He ... he didn't deserve to go out like that."

"*He sure didn't.*"

Jan looks at Ragnar again, and Ragnar mouths a single word: *Hvor?*

"Look, uhm, where are you at?" Jan asks.

"*I'm close,*" Kjell says simply.

"Close to where?"

"*Where you are, of course. The old guy's cave.*"

Jan looks up at Ragnar. Ragnar shakes his head once.

"No, that ... that's not where I am," he says. "I left after I killed the guy."

"*You did?*"

"Yeah. I've been trying to find you."

"*You could have just called me.*"

"Yeah." Jan laughs nervously. "I realized that as soon as you called me. I'd completely forgotten the phone was in the backpack."

Kjell doesn't answer. Judging from his calm voice and lack of other noises, Kristoffer gets the impression he's not moving. Wherever he is, he's probably either standing or sitting. He's focusing on the conversation. Listening to Jan's words and tone. Trying to get a read on him.

On the surface, the way Jan is anxiously babbling would probably come off as dishonest to most people. But then again, the guy seems to always be at least somewhat on edge. And having just been through a shootout, where he—supposedly—shot a guy in cold blood, that wouldn't make it all too implausible that he's extra flustered. Maybe Kjell is thinking the same. Maybe he's buying it.

"Look, if you tell me where you are, I can come to you," Jan goes on. "We can still make it to Russia."

"*I've got a better idea,*" Kjell says plainly. "*Why don't you put the old guy on?*"

Jan's chewing speeds up even more as he looks pleadingly up at Ragnar. "What? No, I told you, he's dead."

"*I wanna speak with him. Give him the phone, Jan.*"

Jan laughs shrilly. "Look, man, I'm telling you, he's dead. So, unless you've got, like, a Ouija board or something, there's no way you're getting anything out of him. Besides, I left the cave already, and I don't know—"

Ragnar calmly takes the phone from Jan, who lets out a hard breath, as though to say: "Thank God."

The old guy places the phone to his ear and says simply: "Ragnar."

Kjell grunts. "*That's your name, huh? Of course it is. It means 'warrior,' did you know that?*"

"We can still call this quits," Ragnar says, getting straight to the point. "You shot one of my guys, I shot one of yours. Fair is fair. We'll let your buddy here walk, and you go on your merry way. How's that?"

"*That's a reasonable suggestion,*" Kjell says calmly. "*Except the guy I shot was a fat, useless nobody. And the guy you shot ... well, he was my brother.*"

"Fair point," Ragnar concedes. "But we have your guy hostage here, so letting him go should tip the scales back to fifty-fifty, wouldn't you say?"

"Jan? That fucking waste of space? He's not worth the air he's breathing. In fact, after he just tried to trick me, I very much plan on killing him along with the rest of you."

"Hey, come on!" Jan shouts. "I was under duress, Kjell! They have a gun to my head!"

Ragnar frowns with annoyance and snaps his fingers, signalling for Jan to shut up. "Look, I get it," he tells Kjell. "Family is different. But there's no need to make it personal. We were only defending ourselves."

"*And now I'm doing the same*," Kjell says, returning to his light-hearted tone. "*I have no guarantee you won't come looking for me. So I need to finish it before I move on.*"

"That's bull crap, and you know it. We just want to be left alone. As far as I'm concerned, our dispute is over."

"*Dispute*," Kjell repeats, chuckling. "*You're a real fucking talker, huh? Brawn **and** brains. Almost wish I could take you with me.*"

"Sorry," Ragnar says. "I'll take my chances right here."

"*I know. That's why I need to come back and turn that cave into a mass grave.*"

"Oh, Jesus," Jan mutters, chewing away frantically. He gets up and looks at Kristoffer. "Look, man. He means business. We need to get the hell away from here."

"Sit down," Ragnar says, not moving the phone from his ear. "And shut the hell up."

Jan rounds on him. He glances towards the cave's opening. For a moment, he looks like he's considering making a run for it.

Ragnar just stares at him, his eyes saying, "Go ahead. Good luck out there."

Jan, picking up on the unspoken message, sits down with a hard breath. He cradles his head, muttering to himself, "We're all fucking dead ..."

"Look," Ragnar says to Kjell. "You sent your brother into the line of fire, and you knew damn well there was a risk. So did he. If you're gonna seek vengeance on anyone who had a role to play in your brother's death, then don't forget yourself."

"*Oh, I won't forgive myself for slipping up,*" Kjell says. "*I know I'm partly complicit. And I'm sure I can live with the guilt. Honestly, I might just blow my own brains out after I've done yours. Would be a relief, to tell you the truth. With the shit I've been through, I'd be happy to put an end to things. Finally stop the nightmares.*"

For the first time, Kristoffer gets the impression Kjell isn't being completely honest. It's not so much the killing himself part that strikes Kristoffer as insincere—he actually sounds like he doesn't fear death or care if his life should end. But the thing about forgiving himself for bearing some responsibility for his brother's death—that part doesn't ring true.

He's not feeling guilty at all, Kristoffer realizes, as a chill runs down his back. *He's got no conscience. He really is a real-life psycho.*

"*So you guys enjoy the last time together in that little cave of yours,*" Kjell goes on. "*Maybe kiss each other goodbye, or suck each other's dicks if that's your flavor. Because I'll be coming back soon to make you—*"

Ragnar abruptly ends the call, handing the satellite phone back to Jan. "I take it that thing can't be traced?"

Jan gapes up at him. "What thing?"

"The phone. Can anyone from the military track it?"

"Uhm, no. We wouldn't have brought it if they could. Hey, why'd you just hang up on him? I guarantee you that just made him more angry."

"Good," Ragnar says simply, going to the shelves where he starts looking through boxes. "The angrier, the rasher. There was nothing more to say. He can't be reasoned with." Ragnar opens a particular box, takes out what looks like a pair of night goggles and throws them to Kristoffer. He sends them both a significant look. "He'll come for us, and we'll need to kill him. So let's get ready."

7

As a little girl, she would often be scared of the boogeyman.

It started when her brothers teased her, telling her that naughty girls would get eaten during the night. Dagny was only four or five at the time, and not nearly old enough to tell facts from fiction. She knew her brothers made up stuff all the time, and she had a suspicion the boogeyman wasn't real. But when it was time for bed, it *felt* real. Very real.

She shared a room with her younger sister, but Kari was always quick to fall asleep, while Dagny tossed and turned. Even if Kari had stayed awake along with her, it would have been a poor comfort, as her sister was always the favorite of their parents.

Dagny was the unruly one. The one that the boogeyman was coming for.

Their house was old and made of wood, and whenever even the slightest wind stirred outside, everything would give off noises. The roof, the walls and especially the cracked old floorboards. It was hard to tell whether it was just the house "settling," as her father called it ... or if someone was hiding below her bed, slowly turning over, trying to be quiet.

Dagny knew no one could be under her bed. At least not anyone very big, because the space down there was stuffed with boxes and bags full of cast-off clothes, blankets, bedsheets and fabric her mother used to sew curtains and tablecloths from.

But Dagny also knew the boogeyman didn't adhere to natural laws. He wasn't a human being; he was more like a demon. No matter how thoroughly she checked the room—including under the bed—during the daytime, she never found him. And yet, as soon as her teeth were brushed, her hair combed and the lights turned off ... there he was. Waiting right below her. And the next morning, when she woke up, squinting against the early sunlight, he would be gone again. Having left the room without opening the door or the window.

She was convinced he would one night pop up, grab her leg and drag her down into the darkness. And there, he would finally eat her alive. He only waited for Dagny to do something bad. To act naughty and give him the excuse he needed to finally feast on her flesh.

Dagny tried very hard to behave. But one day, coming back from milking the cow, she tripped on the cobblestone in the courtyard and spilled the entire bucket.

She was mortified.

The cats came rushing to lick up the puddle, as Dagny just stood there, frozen in place, her mind reeling.

She couldn't let Mom find out. She would tell Dad as soon as he got home from working in the field, and he would whip her for being so uncareful.

So, she ran all the way to their neighbors. They had a bigger farm with more cattle. The older boy was busy cleaning out the stable, and both doors were open. Dagny snuck in from the back and quickly milked the nearest cow. She then went back home with the fresh bucket of milk. Her mother scolded her for taking so long, but she didn't suspect anything.

Dagny got away with it. She steered clear of the whipping.

But she couldn't fool the boogeyman. He knew. And that night, he finally had his excuse to come and eat her.

Dagny was petrified. She almost retched when she brushed her teeth. She peed three times because her bladder kept feeling like it was full.

When she finally went to the room, Kari was snoring away.

Dagny couldn't do it. She couldn't go to bed. The moment she did, she would be grabbed and dragged away.

Instead, she looked to the big old closet by the opposite wall. It was white and had a round mirror fixed to the left-side door. Dagny slipped across the floor. As she opened the closet and crawled inside, she heard a noise from behind and almost screamed out. Looking back, she saw the corner of her duvet hanging out over the edge of the bed. It hadn't done so just a moment ago; Dagny was sure of it. Mom was always meticulous with making their beds.

And in the darkness below the bed, she could swear she saw a pair of shiny black eyes staring out at her.

Dagny yelped and closed the door. Sitting inside the closet among the coats and dresses, the sounds were mercifully muffled, and the familiar smells filled her nose. She felt safe. For the first time in months. She leaned sideways and drifted off almost immediately.

The next morning, her butt was sore and her neck hurt, but she had survived the night, and that was all that mattered. The sun was coming up, and the boogeyman had left again, empty-handed.

From that day on, whenever Dagny slipped up and did something bad, she would spend the night in the closet. She did so until she was thirteen and had to go live on another farm to work and earn money for her parents.

Now, her parents are dead. So are her brothers. And Kari. Dagny is the last one alive, and at 93, she probably doesn't have long left.

She never expected the boogeyman to return. To come back for her. To show up again and claim what he'd been cheated out of all those years ago.

But when she woke up in the early hours of the day to the sound of screaming and fighting from the hallway, Dagny knew instantly that her childhood monster had come for her.

She got out from under the covers. Even for her age, she could move impressively well—her body wasn't affected by the dementia, only her mind—and she slipped across the floor to listen by the door.

What she heard left no trace of doubt. She looked around her room, even though she knew it intimately after having stayed here for—how long? A year? Two? Ten? She could no longer keep track of time. There were no hiding places. No closets. Instead, she headed for the terrace door, grabbing her woollen sweater from off the armchair. Pulling it over her shoulders, her opened the door and stepped out into the freezing cold air.

Shivering, she looked around, trying to decide where to go. She wasn't completely sure where she was, but she knew she'd seen the frozen lawn and the houses on the other side before. The street was empty at this hour, still lit by lampposts. She went left, headed for the parking lot. As she crossed the windows to the last apartment, the glass suddenly exploded.

Dagny screamed and tripped over her own legs.

"Help!" a deep voice roared out. "Help me!"

A heavy guy with an even heavier moustache was trying to climb out of the broken window. He cut himself badly, and his hands began bleeding. The look of terror on his face made Dagny sick to her stomach, and she instinctively drew back, crawling backwards across the frozen ground.

At first, she didn't understand what drove the man to hurt himself like that. But then she saw it. Big hands, grabbing him from behind. One of them wrapped itself around his chest, the other latched onto his face, the fingers slipping into his open mouth as they yanked him back hard. The light in the man's apartment was dim, so the scenery was mostly a silhouette. Yet Dagny couldn't help but see the figure behind the poor guy as it wrestled his head to the side and bit down hard on his neck, turning his scream from panic to pain.

It's really him. He's come to eat me.

Dagny found herself getting to her feet, even though her legs felt like spaghetti. She staggered on, wanted to get as far away from the boogeyman as she could. Turning the corner, she got a clean look of the glass doors by the entrance. In the hall, people were still running and screaming.

He's attacking everyone. But it's me he's come for.

Dagny knew it would be suicide to venture back inside the building. Even the staff—which must by now be aware of the monster that had come to kill her—couldn't do anything to protect her. So, she ran across the lot, headed for the sidewalk. Stumbling down the street, she felt the icy air making her lungs prickle from the inside, and within only a few yards, she almost keeled over from exhaustion.

She was way too old to be running around. Especially in this kind of weather. She had to seek refuge. Find someplace to hide.

She had stopped next to the house neighboring the place where she lived. The lights were on, meaning the people in there were probably awake. They also couldn't help her against the boogeyman, but at least they could let her inside. On the mailbox was a shiny brass sign saying Gunnar, Greta and Marit. So, she ran through the garden, and she stopped in surprise as she found the terrace door wide open. She hesitated, stared into a beautiful living room with expensive furniture. The only thing ruining the pretty impression was a trail of blood drops leading either in or out of the house. Looking down, Dagny saw half of a shoeprint from someone who'd stepped in the blood. The print was facing the street, meaning that whoever had been bleeding had left the house.

What happened here? Was the boogeyman looking for me here first?

She couldn't know for sure. Maybe she would be better off finding somewhere else to—

A scraping noise from behind made her spin around.

That's when she saw him. She'd dreamed of him before, had seen him over a hundred times in her nightmares, but she'd never actually seen him, so she really had no idea what to expect. She assumed he was at least somewhat human in his features, and that much is true. In fact, he looks kinda like the man with the moustache she just saw. His outstretched hands are even cut to bloody shreds. His mouth is hanging open, and most of his cheek is gone, revealing the yellow molars and lolling tongue. His eyes are exactly as she remembers. Black, shiny, soulless.

She realizes in a flash that the boogeyman must be able to jump from body to body. Perhaps that's why it wanted to get her all those years. It wanted to take her over. To walk around in her skin. And now that it had possessed the man with the moustache, its next stop was Dagny.

She spun around and ran into the house, not bothering to close the door behind her. Calling out for someone—anyone—but receiving no reply, she came through a part of the house where fighting had obviously gone down. Then she found herself at the bottom of a staircase, and she ran upstairs. Hyperventilating, she went all the way to the room at the end, which was a bedroom. There were no more doors. No more places to run.

But there was a closet. A big, white one with double doors, just like the closet in her childhood home.

Dagny crossed the floor, opened the closet and crawled inside.

She sat there, hugged her knees, breathed in the smell of fabric softener, stared at the vertical line of dim light coming in, and she felt strangely safe. She had reached her sanctuary, and the closet would once again protect her from the boogeyman as it did so many times in the past.

At least she dearly hopes so.

Listening to the dragging footsteps coming down the hallway, Dagny begins muttering under her breath, not even aware that she's talking out loud, "I'm sorry I spilled the milk. I'm sorry. I didn't mean to. I'm really sorry ..."

8

Pushing through the trees, the leafless branches scratch his hands, and Hagos regrets not grabbing his jacket before leaving Edith's apartment. In its pockets were his gloves and beanie, and he could really use them now. But of course, with how fast things had happened, he should be happy that he even got out of there alive.

That much couldn't be said about Edith or the fat man.

Marit, on the other hand, is somewhere up ahead, and as he stumbles out onto the sidewalk, he's surprised to find the street empty. Well, not entirely empty. A car is parked halfway on the sidewalk. Inside it is trapped an infected woman, who's clawing away at the window. A little farther down, two infected people are eating some poor soul lying on his back.

As though sensing Hagos, they lift their heads in unison and turn in his direction. The morning has almost turned into day, and even from this distance, it's now light enough that Hagos can see their black eyes pin him down. His stomach feels like it's quickly filling up with ice, and he begins jogging in the opposite direction.

Marit got maybe ninety seconds worth of a head start as Hagos fought her father with the lawn mower. She must have come this way, and he has a hard time believing she would have voluntarily passed by the two infected people.

"Marit?" he calls out, looking in every direction.

No answer comes. At least not in the form of words. Across the street is a line of buildings, and from the carport of one of them comes a woman who's almost naked. She's in her fifties and a little heavy. Her skin is white as snow, starkly contrasted by the dark-red, gaping holes that have been dug in her chest, abdomen and shoulder. It looks like they caught her coming out of the shower, because her hair is still wet, clinging to her face, and her bra is only covering one breast. She's not wearing any underpants, revealing a dark strip of pubic hair.

Hagos feels both horrified and embarrassed for her, and quickly looks away.

He continues down the street in a light jog, keeps scanning all around to make sure no one sneaks up on him. Somewhere, someone screams. A few blocks over, a gun is fired several times. More screaming. It doesn't sound like someone in physical pain—more like someone who just witnessed something gruesome. Perhaps the death of a loved one. Hagos feels deeply empathetic with whoever is screaming.

"Marit?" he calls out again.

As he still doesn't receive an answer, he decides that the girl is lost to him. She obviously didn't wait around, and perhaps that's for the best. She wasn't exactly working well under pressure, and he can't imagine having her around would be much of a help right now. In fact, she would probably be more of a liability.

Where do I go?

The obvious answer is that he needs to get as far out of town as possible, and to do that, he needs a vehicle. He can't get to his car, which is parked on the other side of the nursing home. Going back there would no doubt be stupid. And he can't exactly call a cab either. The authorities must be very much aware of the situation by now—he can hear sirens a few blocks over, along with more gunshots—but they've probably got their hands full in dealing with the infected, so expecting them to offer him an escort in a crisis situation like this isn't realistic.

Hagos stops as he reaches an adjacent street. He has three choices. Well, two, because behind him is a tall wooden fence, and the way he just came is now blocked by the woman along with the two other infected people, all of whom are still coming for him. So he can either proceed down the road, which will take him closer to the centrum of town, or he can choose the adjacent street, which will lead deeper into the residential area. Both are bad choices. Both are heavily populated. Both are very likely crawling with infected people—if not yet, then it's just a matter of minutes.

His best bet might be the residential area, because beyond that are the outskirts of town.

And Juma. His friend lives in an apartment complex in that direction.

The infected probably didn't reach that far yet. If only Hagos had some way of getting there. Making the trip by foot would take at least half an hour, even if he jogs. But for now, he has no other choice, so he's about to cross the street when he hears an engine coming this way, fast.

A car approaches. Whoever's driving is really gunning it, plus they're swerving dangerously this way then that. They clip a thin rowan tree standing between the road and the sidewalk. It can't withstand the force of the car, and the frozen stem snaps and slams over the roof of the car. The impact is hard enough to cause the airbags to deploy, and in a flash, the face behind the wheel is covered by a white pillow. The car goes skidding out of control, and racing across the street, it hits a lamppost—which doesn't give way as easily as the young tree. The sound of metal against metal rings out, hitting Hagos's eardrums with a painful jab.

Then the sound is replaced with a siren coming this way. People inside the car—Hagos realizes there are at least two in the backseat—all begin scrambling to get out.

A police car comes racing, slamming its brakes, and two cops job out just as the people in the crashed car tumble out and take flight on foot. One of them—a young guy—is limping. At first, Hagos takes it to be from the crash, but then he sees the next guy, also a young fellow, who's clutching a makeshift bandage on his upper arm. It looks like a dishtowel he wrapped with a shoelace, and blood is soaking through the fabric. The third guy, the one who was driving, pops out with a bloody nose—this one most likely did happen in the crash—and he immediately grabs the guy with the bad foot and hoists him along.

"Come on, man," he wheezes. "Hurry up!"

"Stop!" one of the officers shouts, pulling out his gun. "Stop, or we will fire!"

Whether it's an empty threat or not, Hagos has no idea, and he doesn't intend to stick around and find out. He finds himself backed up against the wooden fence, and without a second thought, he turns around, jumps up and scales it before anyone takes notice of him.

As he lands in a neatly kept garden, he hears the driver shout back to the cops: "No, don't! We told you, we're not infected!"

"This is your last warning!" the cop replies.

Then, three seconds later, the threat turns out to have been real enough. Because bullets start flying.

Hagos heads for the house.

9

"I'd like to switch."

Aksel sits up with a grunt as the cop nudges his leg. "Huh?" He looks around, seeing nothing much except a frozen landscape in the late afternoon light. "Oh, right." He rubs his eye and yawns. "I'm up?"

Anne glances back. "She finally fell asleep just ten minutes ago. Would be a shame to wake her up now."

Aksel looks to the backseat. Coiled up on the right is Rosa, sleeping peacefully. Belinda is sitting next to her, leaning over her daughter. Her eyes are closed, but her forehead is still creased. It took her a long time to stop worrying that Rosa was okay, that she wasn't going to die from hyperthermia or had suffered a minor scratch somewhere that would slowly spread the infection throughout her system. Finally, after they'd driven for half an hour and left Trondheim behind, she relented and stopped feeling Rosa's forehead every other minute. Rosa had already fallen asleep from exhaustion by then, and Aksel soon drifted off too.

"What time is it now?" he mutters, checking the clock in the dashboard.

"It's been five hours, if that's what you mean," Anne says, pulling over by the wayside. There's a patch of trees visibly crooked from growing against the wind. "I think she would have spiked a fever by now."

Aksel unbuckles. "That's great news."

Getting out of the MPV, the cold, crisp country air immediately causes him to shiver. Now that the sun is hidden behind the trees on the horizon, the temperature is dropping rapidly. Had the incident with Rosa being trapped under the car taken place at this time of day, the cold might just have killed her. As he goes around the back of the car, he glances in at the girl. Her legs are mostly hidden under her mom's blouse which she's using as a blanket, but he can see a small area on the back of her upper thigh. Her skin is awfully pale—as is everyone's skin around here at this time of year, unless they go to a tanning salon thrice a week—so the blue bruise is all the more visible. It's from where she touched the frozen asphalt, and it has thin, red lines running across it. It looks normal, and already better.

She'll be fine. Thank God.

Aksel would have had a hard time forgiving himself if Rosa hadn't made it.

As he comes around to the other side of the car, a glow catches his eye on the northern horizon. Getting in behind the wheel, he points ahead. "Is that Mo coming up?"

"It is," Anne says, looking intently at her seat belt as she buckles up.

Oh, Aksel thinks. *That's why she wanted me to take over.*

Anne told them about her daughter. He couldn't begin to imagine how awful she must feel, having just lost her only child. At least she got to say goodbye to her, even though it was only over the phone. Belinda could obviously relate—she teared up when Anne relayed the story, and then Belinda asked where the girl's father was.

"She hasn't got one," was all Anne said to that.

Aksel is surprised she's still able to function. She obviously had no other family than her daughter, and now she's all alone.

Then again, that's exactly the position Aksel himself is in. Jakob was, for all intents and purposes, his only family. At least the only family he cared for. Their dad was still alive somewhere, but Aksel couldn't even bring himself to call him. And then there was Frida, of course. They hadn't been dating for long, but Aksel was falling for her big time when she was torn away too.

How are we able to carry on? Aksel wonders. *We should be balled up in a corner, crying.*

Perhaps it would come later. As a delayed response. When they've finally found someplace safe, where they can rest and relax, and not be in constant danger. Aksel has always been good at shoving things aside. And he suspects Anne is the same way. She strikes him as a very disciplined woman. Strong. Not prone to giving into her emotions.

Still, ever since they left Trondheim, he can tell she's pulling deeper and deeper into herself. She only talks when someone asks her something. Most of the time, she seems lost to the world.

"So," he says, adjusting the mirrors. "We should probably go around town, right?"

Anne shifts her gaze from the seat belt to the radio, still firmly avoiding looking ahead. "Uh-huh. They've been talking nonstop about how it's spiraling. The part of town where—" She cuts herself off, clears her throat. "That particular part of town has been sealed off. But I'm sure they're also busy blocking all the major roads going in and out of town. So, we stick to the smaller roads and we steer clear. Last thing we want is getting pulled over."

"Yeah, we tried that already," Aksel mutters. "All right, let's get—"

He's just released the handbrake and is about to drive on, when he suddenly catches a face staring at him from between the branches of a young, leafless pussy willow. At first glance, he takes it to be a wolf. Aksel has seen plenty of wolves on his hunting trips, and the pale blue eyes fixed on him at that moment sure remind him of that. The color of the fur is greyish, leaning towards brown, and it's visibly ruffled, as though the animal has been tearing through bushes. However, this face isn't framed by a thick winter-mane, and the ears are floppy, not pointy. But the biggest giveaway is that the animal is at least a full head too tall to be a wolf.

"Look," Aksel mutters, squinting. "See that? I think ... it's a dog."

He puts the handbrake back on and opens his door without breaking eye-contact with the animal.

"We don't know if it's friendly," Anne reminds him.

"I'm going to find out," Aksel says, stepping out of the car. "Hey, boy. You okay?"

The dog's ears move, revealing that it hears his voice. It doesn't do anything else; it just keeps standing there, peeking through the branches.

"It's wearing a collar," Anne remarks. "That means it's someone's dog, and they could be nearby."

"I don't think they are," Aksel says, looking around. "There are no houses out here. And look at the guy's fur. He's been either chasing or fleeing from something. Judging by how timid he looks, I'm betting the latter."

"All the more reason to leave him be," Anne argues. "Damn thing is big enough to kill you."

"Yeah," Aksel mutters. "It is."

From what he can see, the dog is a mixed breed. Aksel isn't an expert, but he's pretty sure it's got some Great Dane in it. Either that, or some other really large breed. There's something about the size of the dog that's intriguing to him. It looks very powerful, but at the same time, even though it's clearly anxious, it also seems friendly. It's not barking, bristling, growling, or showing its teeth. It's just standing there; watching, waiting.

"You cold, buddy?" Aksel asks, taking a few steps closer. He leaves the door open, in case he needs to dive back inside the car, but he tries his best to look and sound casual. "I don't really have any treats to offer you, but the car is warm if you want to come along."

Anne opens her own door and sticks her head out. "What are you doing? Why would you bring along some stray dog?"

Aksel glances back, placing a finger over his lips. "Please, keep it down. Don't scare him off." He throws out his arms—which causes the dog to startle, and he immediately regrets it. In a low voice, he tells Anne: "You said it yourself. He's big enough to take down a person. Don't you think a friend like that could come in handy?"

Anne finally catches on. She says in a tone that's not fully convinced, but also not really caring: "We already have a gun."

"Guns run out of ammo," Aksel mutters, kneeling. "This guy won't. Here, boy! You wanna say hi?" He holds out his palms, showing them empty.

The dog reacts by lifting its head. It apparently picks up on a sound, because it breaks eye-contact for the first time in order to look to the side.

Aksel follows its gaze. In the distance, there are more trees. A forest, in fact. It's probably where the dog came from. If it used to live over there, it doesn't look at all interested in going back.

Aksel glances towards the town up ahead. "How far from Mo are we?" he asks Anne, not looking back.

"Fifteen minutes, I guess. You think the dog came from town?"

"No," Aksel mutters. "I think it's much more likely he lived out here somewhere, with some old hermit. But I'm wondering if something else has come from town ..."

He can all too vividly imagine someone escaping Mo before the roadblocks were properly in place. All it took was one infected person, one little scratch hidden under a pant leg or a sleeve, and the quarantine was compromised. It wasn't hard to think of a scenario in which someone had driven out here, only to die behind the wheel, then wake back up and wander off to find the nearest prey—some poor old guy living alone with his giant dog.

When the dog turned its head, Aksel saw something blue at the corner of its mouth. The lower lip is black and drooping, and the blue thing appear to be a piece of fabric. Anne doesn't seem to have noticed, and Aksel doesn't want to tell her. The dog has obviously been in a fight where it had to bite someone, and if Anne knew that, she'd likely take the wheel and drive off with or without Aksel.

But Aksel's gut still tells him the dog is friendly. He doesn't believe it bit anyone out of aggression, but finds it much more likely it did so because it was forced to defend itself.

"You're a good boy, aren't you?" he asks, making the dog look at him again. "You're just scared and freezing. Really wish I had something to offer you …" He recalls the water bottle that sat in the cupholder. It was frozen solid when they turned on the car, but after having been driving with the heater at full blast, it's thawed out. Aksel goes back to the car. He grabs the bottle and goes a little closer to the trees. He crouches down and unscrews the cap. The dog is eyeing him intently. "You thirsty? I've got some water here …"

He pours out a tiny amount, just enough for the dog to see. It raises its ears and reflexively takes a step sideways, revealing its body. It's even bigger than Aksel thought. It's also in worse shape. It's meaty chest is full of twigs, the fur has been pulled this way then that, and it's even missing patches here and there.

For a moment, Aksel considers if the dog could have been bitten. It might even be infected.

Then he recalls the cat back at Linus's garage. He mutters to himself: "They're not interested in animals."

Even if it was an infected person who attacked the dog and not just tree branches, he feels fairly certain the dog won't die and wake up as a zombie. In *The Walking Dead*, the rules were very clear: Animals aren't affected by the virus.

Still, should he risk his own life based on a TV show? Worse, should he risk the lives of Rosa, Belinda and Anne?

Aksel can't really tell why he's so enamored with this dog. He does think it could make a great protector—if it's willing to come with them and maybe in time come to think of them as its new owners, that is. But it's more than that. Perhaps it just seems like fate that they should happen to meet each other out here in the middle of nowhere. After all, the odds are pretty damn small. Had they stopped three minutes prior or driven on for just one more mile, they would have missed the dog entirely.

But they didn't. They pulled over right here, where it was standing, hiding, waiting.

Aksel has always been fond of dogs. They had a cocker spaniel growing up, and both he and Jakob were heartbroken when it got bone cancer and had to be put down. Their dad didn't want to get a new one. Ever since Aksel moved out, he had wanted to get his own dog, he just couldn't make it fit with working twelve-hour shifts at the hospital. Then he met Frida and forgot all about it.

And now, as the world is about to end, he finds himself eye to eye with a dog who's very likely lost its owners and will freeze to death before dawn.

If that's not destiny, Aksel doesn't know what is.

As though to confirm it, the dog steps all the way out from behind the trees and comes towards him. It does so in a slinky, almost apologetic manner; head down, ears flat, tail whipping from side to side. Aksel knows this kind of body language from a dog can mean one of two things. Either it's scared and defensive, and he should back off—or it's friendly and submissive. He's willing to gamble on the latter, so he pours a little water into his cupped hand and holds it out.

The dog barely sniffs it before it plunges its huge snout into his hand and begins lapping eagerly, causing most of the water to splash out. The dog is really big up close; with Aksel crouching, they're eye-to-eye.

"Whoa, you're really thirsty, huh? Here you go …" Aksel pours more water into his hand. The dog doesn't stop drinking until the bottle is empty. Then it laps its soaked lips and snout, and, looking up at Aksel, it leans in and places a big, wet kiss on his chin. Aksel pulls back, grinning. "You're welcome!"

As though hearing an invitation in his voice, the dog comes forward and burrows its huge head under his arm, causing him to lose balance. He lands on his ass with a grunt and begins petting the dog. It acts like it wants to climb into his lap, even though it's obviously way too big.

He checks the brass tag on the collar. It says simply, Guardian. There is no other information. No owner's name, no address, or phone number. Which, if he's being honest, Aksel is relieved. He doesn't want to return Guardian to its owners—even if they are still alive, which he doubts—and now, that option is out.

He gets to his feet, and as the dog is still rubbing against him, demanding more affection, he turns his head to look back at Anne with a grin.

She's sitting with her arms crossed, her eyes distant. Then she seems to notice him, and she shrugs indifferently, as though saying, "Okay, you win; now can we get going, please?"

10

The house appears to be empty—at least there are no lights on in there.

Which Hagos finds curious.

Haven't the residents heard anything? They live only one house over from the nursing home, and this whole thing started hours ago. Even if they've somehow managed to ignore all the noise of sirens, screams and gunshots, they must at least have gazed out their windows, which on the north side all seem to face the street he just came from. Hagos finds it unlikely whoever is in the house hasn't caught on to what's going on. It's much more probably they either turned off the lights to not attract attention and then hunkered down in their basement, or maybe they simply upped and left, packed a suitcase and drove the hell away. He would consider that the smart thing to do.

There's another possibility, of course. A much less happy outcome for the people living here. And as he comes around to the driveway, he sees several things pointing to that theory. The front door is open. The car is still there—its door is open, too. No one's inside. Well, if you don't count the Chihuahua sitting on the passenger seat, shivering. It's wearing a coat with a leash attached to it. The other end of the leash is lying on the pavement outside the car.

The dog looks at him with scared eyes and shows its teeth in what could be a welcoming grin or a threatening sneer. Either way, Hagos never cared for dogs—big or small—so he wasn't intending to go any closer. On the ground next to the leash is also a pair of slippers. They aren't left carefully there, as you do when you step out of them, but have obviously been dropped in a hurry. One is upside down, the other is kicked halfway under the car.

The biggest giveaway that something bad happened here, however, is the pool of blood by the front tire. It has also stained the silvery rims. He steps over there. The Chihuahua begins growling at him, and he's glad he didn't go to it. Instead, he carefully dips the toe of his shoe in the blood. As he suspected, it's frozen solid. Which means it's been at least thirty minutes before it was spilled. Plenty of time for whoever was bleeding to die, wake back up, and waddle off to find fresh prey.

In his mind, Hagos replays what very likely happened here.

The owner—a man, judging by the size of the slippers—came out with the dog on the leash, wanting to let it have a quick morning pee on the lawn, when an infected person showed up and surprised them both. A scuffle ensued, in which the man lost his slippers, tried to get inside the car for safety, but ultimately got overpowered and killed. As he later left, the dog must have decided to not follow along, instead jumping into the car.

Hagos looks to the open front door. Could he be lucky enough to find the keys for the car inside? Or will he only find someone infected, roaming the rooms in search of someone to eat?

Hagos steps closer and listens. He's pretty sure anyone infected wouldn't stick around an empty house, not with the front door open. As soon as they realized there was nothing to eat, they would press on, seek prey somewhere else.

So, he steps into the entrance hall and holds his breath. There are still background noises from the city, but nothing from inside the house. It's not much warmer in here than outside, which confirms to him that it's been a while since the owner left his house. Hagos leaves the front door open as he checks for the car key. He was hoping to find it on the foyer table, but there are only a vase and some ugly figurine from Norse mythology. Judging by the shoes and coats, the man could have been living here alone. At least there are no women's or children's outerwear.

He moves towards the opening which leads into a big, white kitchen. It looks clean enough. No signs of any fighting. No blood, nothing knocked to the floor. Either the guy had house cleaning, or he was very cleanly himself, because everything veritably shines.

And right there, on the kitchen counter, lies a big key chain. One of them is for a Nissan.

"Yes," Hagos mutters, grabbing the bundle.

He can't believe his luck. He's actually getting out of here, and completely unharmed. His ticket is parked right outside. Whatever legal consequences he might face for taking the vehicle probably won't be severe considering the circumstances. The important thing is that he can drive away from town and find somewhere to—

He's about to turn and leave, when a movement catches his eye through the window. There's a nice view of the man's garden. What has caught Hagos's eyes, however, is something in the house next door. It has one of those floor-to-ceiling windows, and through it, Hagos can see the stairs leading to the second floor. A young woman at the top of the stairs is talking to someone on her cell phone, pacing back and forth on the landing.

"Marit," Hagos whispers.

Then he sees another movement. There's light in the downstairs kitchen windows. At that moment, a man walks by, headed for the stairs. Even from over here, Hagos can tell he's most definitely dead.

And Marit, apparently, has no idea he's coming for her.

11

It's weird. She's freezing and sweating at the same time. Almost like a fever.

Something's wrong with her right arm; it's not responding when she tries to move it. It must be broken or something. But weirdly, it doesn't hurt. And it's not just her arm; her entire body seems to be pinned in place, making her unable to move. She can smell oil, rubber and asphalt. She can hear the zombies growling and grunting.

Oh, no. I'm still trapped under the car, she realizes with a sinking feeling of horror.

She was sure she'd escaped. That she's safe inside the car with her mother and Aksel and the cop. But apparently, that was just a dream. Something her mind conjured up. Likely because it was too scared to handle the situation.

Did I pass out? I must have.

She tries very hard to open her eyes, but it's difficult. She's very tired. One of the zombies must be very close, because she can smell its rancid breath hit her face. She tries to scream, but it only comes out as a whimper.

"Rosa!"

Her mother's voice, somewhere close. She must be calling for her from inside the car.

Rosa tries to call back, tries to pull away from the zombie, which is coming even closer now. It's sniffing eagerly and making wet noises too, as though licking its lips.

"It's okay, Rosa!" Mom reassures her. Then, seemingly addressing someone else: "Can you get that thing to back off? It's scaring her."

Rosa has no idea whom Mom is talking to, but she finds it very strange that she thinks anyone has the authority to command a zombie to go away.

To her surprise, though, Aksel's voice comes from somewhere nearby: "Down, boy. Look, it's okay, he just wants to sniff her …"

The zombie is very close now, grunting and drooling right next to Rosa's ear, and she's really panicking, trying with all her might to wake up properly, to get her body to react. It's only when the zombie licks her ear with a tongue that seems way too big and sloppy that she's finally able to scream out and open her eyes.

"Jesus!" Mom says. "It's okay, Rosa! You just had a bad dream …"

Rosa stares around, at first not comprehending at all what her eyes are telling her. She's not under the car, but inside it, lying on the backseat. What's constricting her movement is partly the blanket that's wrapped around her, partly her mother, who's trying to hold her. Her right arm really isn't moving, but that's only because she's been lying on it, causing it to fall asleep.

The car is moving. It's dark outside, which means they must have been going for several hours. The female cop is turned in her seat, looking back at her with mild concern, and Aksel is behind the wheel.

"Is she awake now?" he asks.

"Yes," Mom says, helping Rosa sit up properly. Her head feels like it's full of water, and the world spins around itself for a moment. "You're okay, honey," Mom reassures her with a smile. "You're safe."

"What … what happened?" Rosa mutters, blinking.

Mom uses the corner of the blanket to wipe Rosa's cheek, and she realizes that it's all wet. That someone really did lick her just now. Rosa is overwhelmed by a strong feeling of not being sure whether she's still asleep; whether this is just another dream that took over from the previous one. Perhaps she's still—

Another grunt. Rosa turns her head. A huge dog is sitting in the cargo area. It's so tall that if it sat upright, its ears would likely be touching the ceiling. But the dog is hunched over, leaning its neck between the headrests. Despite its size, the dog looks very friendly, almost goofy. The pink tongue is lolling as it's trying to reach her to place another dog kiss on her face.

"Whose ... whose dog is that?" Rosa asks, still not sure this is real—though she's starting to feel more awake.

"It's Aksel's," Mom says. "He picked him up while we were sleeping. I almost peed myself when I woke up and saw him." That last part she says while sending Aksel a look.

"It's not *my* dog," Aksel says, glancing back. "He's *our* dog. His name is Guardian. He's part of the family now."

The cop grunts, but doesn't say anything.

"Guardian," Rosa repeats.

The dog reacts by lifting its ears. Rosa holds up her hand, wanting to pat his head, but he instead slobbers all over it. It tickles, and she snickers.

"He likes you," Aksel says.

"He likes everyone," Mom remarks. "I'm really not sure he'll be much of a guardian ..."

"Don't write him off too soon," Aksel says. "He might seem like a big kid, but my gut tells me he'll do what's necessary if push comes to shove."

The dog stops licking her palm and instead nudges her with his snout, so she scratches him behind the ear—which is bigger than her hand.

Rosa has barely had time to come to terms with the fact that Garfield is gone—likely forever. When they got detained, the cops wouldn't let her bring the cat. She had to simply let him go. He wasn't exactly upset about it; he'd always preferred quiet and solitude, so all the sirens and people and buzz were a bit much for him, and he quickly slinked away. Garfield had always been a very independent cat. Often he would prowl the town at night, and it wasn't unusual for three or four days to pass before he decided to come home again. Then, after a week or so, he'd take off again. So Rosa isn't worried he'll be fine. He can take care of himself. It just makes her sad that she probably won't see him again.

And now here's a new pet. Rosa always wanted a dog, but Linus was allergic—he could barely tolerate Garfield. Rosa feels tears well up into her eyes, and she suddenly begins crying. It's not a breakdown; not a reaction to the traumatic experience she had being trapped under the car. It's much softer, deeper. She's overwhelmed by a feeling of grief, of loss, of having had loved ones torn away. Linus, Helen, Garfield.

"Oh, honey," Mom says, pulling her into a hug. "It's all right now. We're safe."

"I know," Rosa tries to say, but the words drown in sobs, and she simply gives in to the embrace and cries for a while.

When the tears subside, she wipes her face and takes a couple of deep breath.

"Feel better?" Mom asks.

"Uh-huh."

"You were very ... brave back there." Mom winces as she swallows. It obviously causes her pain, though she tries to hide it. "I'm proud of you, honey."

"Are you okay, Mom?" Rosa asks, surveying her face.

"Sure. It's just the mono acting up."

"Oh."

"The what now?" Aksel asks, looking up at the mirror.

"I've got mono," Mom mutters, swallowing again, giving a grunt of pain. "It acts up whenever I'm stressed out. Makes my throat sore as hell."

"Well, we should get you some painkillers," Aksel says. "Why didn't you say something earlier?"

"Painkillers don't really work anyway," Mom shrugs. "But it's fine. It'll go away again, eventually."

Rosa remembers three or four times in the past where Mom's illness flared up. One time was when she got fired just before Christmas. And after her breakup with the guy she was with before Linus. Last time, when it got bad, a rash broke out on her back, and she was in bed with a fever for a few days. This situation is considerably worse. Fighting for your life, almost losing your daughter—that was way more stressful than being unemployed over the holidays or having some guy break up with you. No wonder the mono was gearing up. Rosa is worried Mom will be in a lot of pain for a long time.

Apparently, Mom senses it, because she smiles at Rosa. "Don't worry about me, honey. I'm fine. Seriously."

Rosa tries to smile back.

Guardian gives a whimper. Rosa turns her head to see him still sitting there, his jaw resting on the seat, his eyes big and solemn. He's obviously upset that she was crying.

"It's okay," Rosa tells him, scratching the bridge of his nose. "You don't need to be sad just because I am."

Guardian just sighs.

Rosa becomes aware of a slight stinging sensation on her thigh. She pulls aside the blanket to reveal her legs. They're both a little roughed-up from lying on the asphalt. She was afraid she would get frostbite—they told them about it at school, and how dangerous it is to be outside in the winter without enough clothes on—but it looks like she got away with a few minor cuts and some bruises.

"Where are we?" Rosa asks, looking out at the dark, hilly landscape.

"We're not far from Torik," Aksel says, his tone turning dark. "Which means we're deep into zombie land. But don't worry, we'll steer clear of any trouble. I know the roads pretty well up here. This way will take us in a big arch around the city. There's basically no one living here. The only other town is a dump called Bodum, but that's like ten houses and one communal crapper."

Rosa can't help but shiver as she gazes out into the darkness. It's all too easy to imagine stray zombies wandering around out there. She can't help but worry; if they crash on the icy road or run out of gas, they'll be forced to leave the car, going back out into the cold.

Her stomach gives a low growl. "Oh, I'm hungry," she says.

Anne bends over and comes up with a clear plastic bag which she hands back.

Rosa takes the bag and sees a selection of snacks of all kinds. From Danishes to Kit Kats to Cheetos. "Holy cow," she mutters. "Where did all this come from?"

"We stopped at a Joker," Aksel explains. "The shelves were already almost empty. All the real food was gone, even the sodas and juices. I brought as much as I could carry. We have enough for a few days."

Rosa takes in the view one more time. She's never seen this much goodness all at once. Her mouth begins watering. She glances at Mom.

"Something wrong?" Mom asks.

"Well ... it's not Friday."

Mom smiles. "I know. We'll make an exception."

She takes a moment to decide. Then she pulls out a Snickers and carefully unwraps it. Taking a huge bite, she enjoys the taste immensely.

A wet noise from behind. Rosa turns to see Guardian eyeing her closely. Saliva is dripping from his mouth.

"I'm sorry," Rosa says, her mouth full of peanuts and caramel. "But I don't think chocolate is good for dogs."

"Don't let him fool you," Aksel grunts. "He already ate a week's worth of calories. Down, boy. Stop begging."

Guardian grunts, licks his lips, but stays where he is, his eyes glued to the candy bar in Rosa's hand.

"Yeah, we'll have to work a little on obedience," Aksel says. "But he's basically a good boy. I think he—"

"Look out."

Anne suddenly speaks up. She doesn't shout, but she sounds very serious.

Aksel immediately slows down. "What? What is it?"

Rosa stretches her neck to look ahead. She can see nothing but the road. They're coming into a slight curve, going around the side of a hill. On the other side runs a crash barrier, preventing cars from going off the road, which would send them flying down a pretty steep slope.

"I saw something blink," Anne says. "There was a reflection in the guardrail. Slow down even more."

Aksel does so, and as they drive around the hill, Rosa is very thankful Anne warned them, or they would likely have plowed right into the bus. It's lying on its side, the undercarriage exposed, blocking most of the narrow road. One of the rear blinkers is still going, which must be what Anne saw.

"Shit," Aksel mutters, coming to a complete stop. "Good catch, Anne."

"Guess someone didn't bother to put on winter tires," Anne mutters grimly.

"Geez," Mom says. "I sure hope it wasn't full of passengers when it crashed."

"Think we can go around?" Aksel asks—Rosa isn't sure exactly who he's addressing, but he's pointing to the narrow gap between the hillside and the front end of the bus. They'll have to drive onto the side of the road, but the space looks like the MPV can just slip through, and even though they'll go off the asphalt, the ground should be frozen solid, so they won't risk getting stuck. When no one answers him, Aksel goes on: "It's worth a shot. Could take us hours to go back and find another road."

He turns onto the side of the road. He drives carefully, and the MPV slowly passes through the gap without scraping against the back of the bus.

"What's that sound?" Rosa asks as she becomes aware of a rhythmical thumping coming from the bus.

"I hear it too," Mom says. "Is the bus's engine still going?"

"No," Aksel mutters, stopping the car. "It's something else … or rather, *someone*."

Rosa turns in her seat. The top of the bus has no windows, and it's too tall for her to see the side windows, which are facing the sky. So she has no way of knowing what's going on inside the bus. But she can still hear the banging sound. It's slightly louder now, but not as consistent anymore. The intervals are growing longer, as though whatever is producing the sound is slowing down or tiring out.

"It could be an infected person," Mom says.

"Most likely," Aksel says.

Mom leans forward. "Then why are you stopping?"

Aksel is leaning over the steering wheel, trying to get a look at the front of the bus, which is pointing out over the valley. "This isn't a regular bus," he mumbles.

"It's a prisoner transport," Anne says.

"Well, all the more reason to not go poking around," Mom says. "Can we please just get going?"

Rosa saw in a comedy movie once where someone was taken off to a prison, and though it was on a bus, it didn't look at all like this one.

The one in front of her looks more like a regular bus, like one of those that tourists use when they head up into the mountains to go skiing.

"Let me just check real quick," Aksel says.

Rosa expects him to open the door and jump out. Instead, he honks the horn.

"What are you doing?" Mom exclaims. "Are you trying to draw their attention? Why would you—"

"Just listen," Aksel cuts her off with a finger across his lips. "You guys hear that?"

They all listen. Rosa can't hear anything. "It's stopped," she says.

"Exactly. That means it was a human doing the banging, not a zombie."

"How can we know for sure?" Mom asks.

"Because, they don't react to sounds," Aksel says right away. "You could fire a gun next to their ear, and they wouldn't give a damn. I'm not even sure their senses are still operating. I think the only thing they go by is some kind of instinct, which tells them—"

"Hello?"

The voice from the bus is hard to hear. Both because the car's engine is going, the heater is on, but also because whoever is calling sounds hoarse, exhausted.

"Who's out there?"

Aksel glances around at them. "Guess that answers it. Someone's alive in there."

12

"Please, Daniel. I really, really need you right now. Can't you just ... tell your parents you're going somewhere else?"

She walks back and forth, pressing the phone to her ear.

"I'm sorry, Marit. They won't let me take the car."

"But it's an emergency," Marit says, breaking into tears again. "Please, Daniel. My mom and dad ... they're both dead ..."

"I know, and I'm really sorry. But I already told you, they barricaded all the roads going in and out of Mo. They're showing it on television right now."

"You can find a way through," Marit insists, sniffling. "There are hiking paths and gravel roads. Surely, they haven't closed all of them."

"I think they have. They're saying it's really serious."

"Of course it's serious! People are dying, Daniel. *I'm* dying! Doesn't that mean anything to you?"

"Of course it does, Marit. There's just no way my parents will—"

"Fine," Marit says, turning icy. "If I die, then it's on you."

"Come on, Ma—"

She ends the call abruptly. She stares at the phone, chewing her lip, hoping that he'll call her back. She's tried everyone she knows within driving distance. None of them could or would come to her help. At first, she tried the local police, but she couldn't even get through. Then she tried 1-1-2, but they told her help was already on sight, and that the best thing she could do was to stay indoors, make sure the doors were locked and keep out of sight.

Marit tried to explain to the woman on the other end that this was a special situation, that both her parents were dead, that she really needed someone to come get her out of here. But the woman didn't get it. She just kept telling her that the police were doing everything they could, and that a lot of people needed help this morning.

Marit didn't care about those other people. None of them had been through what she had been through. She had survived not only one but two life-threatening situations. She was an even bigger victim than those poor kids who died at the Uttoya shootings. Surely she deserved to be rescued right away. When she told the woman that, the stupid cow simply began repeating what she'd already said four or five times, so Marit cursed at her and hung up.

It didn't matter that the authorities couldn't be counted on; she felt certain her closest friends would come to her aid.

And now, she's been through everyone she could think of. All of them already knew about what was going down in Mo. None of them wanted to come help her.

What's wrong with people?

Marit never imagined her friends could be this selfish. She thought they had a little more humanity. That they'd at the very least—

"Ow!" She hisses as her ankle gives off a painful jab. She sits down on the landing and rubs it. The swelling has gotten worse. She really shouldn't be walking on it. It probably dislocated when Ella pushed her from the window. What was she thinking? Marit could have broken her neck. She feels bad for her cousin. After all, she's dead now. But that doesn't mean you can go shoving people from the second floor. Anyone with a little sense of decency would have never—

Marit hears a noise from downstairs and turns her head towards the stairs. Someone is coming up the steps.

"Oh, thank God," Marit exclaims, almost bursting into tears of relief. Someone decided to come for her after all. "I'm up here!"

She's about to get up to see who it is, but then she changes her mind. She'll appear more vulnerable if she stays down, and the last thing she wants is for whoever is coming to get the impression that she didn't really need their help after all.

"Thank you so much!" she says, still on the verge of crying. "You saved my life. I can't tell you how grateful I am …"

The person isn't answering. They're apparently just focused on scaling the stairs.

Marit frowns. She closed the front door, she's sure of it. The infected people can't open doors.

Still, something about how the person doesn't say anything makes her nervous. She reaches up, grabs the railing and pulls herself up.

She sees the dead guy coming up the stairs, and she tries to scream, but everything inside of her freezes. The dead guy is tall, gangly and bald. His age is difficult to tell, because most of his face is gone. His nose and lips have been gnawed down, both eyes dug out, and even the skin on his forehead was ripped off, including the eyebrows. Marit once saw a haunting picture of a person who'd been caught in a burning building and wasn't saved in time. The poor guy had been reduced to a bloody, featureless mess. This is what the person coming towards her looks like. The only difference is, of course, fire didn't do this; teeth did.

Marit tries to stand up, but her knees buckle, and she slumps back down onto her ass. Instead, she begins kicking, scooching backwards away from the stairs.

As the infected guy reaches the landing, a face appears between his legs—a face Marit knows.

"Hagos!"

The Black guy grabs both of the guy's ankles and pulls hard enough for him to fall flat on the landing. The guy is so tall, his outstretched hands actually reach Marit, slamming down on her shins. He immediately begins groping her, and Marit screams and kicks. The guy catches her foot, yanks it closer and bites down hard on her toes. Marit's thankful that she had enough wit to put on her sneakers when she returned to the house. If she hadn't, the guy would have no doubt bitten her toes clean off.

Instead, he only gets a taste of leather and rubber, and as he's suddenly dragged backwards, the shoe comes free and follows along.

Marit sees Hagos pulling at the guy's legs from behind, forcing him back towards the stairs. Still on his stomach, fumbling with the shoe, the infected guy doesn't have much time to react. He drops the shoe and tries to turn over, but Hagos grabs his belt and yanks one more time, sending him tumbling down the steps. He snarls, grabs for Hagos and manages to catch his thigh and almost pull him along. But Hagos grabs the railing with both hands, and the infected guy loses his grip and goes tumbling head over heels.

Marit stares at Hagos as the guy gets to his feet and checks his palms, then his leg where the zombie grabbed him. Finally, he looks at Marit. "You OK?"

"I'm ... fine," she croaks. "How did you ...? Where did you ...?"

"I saw you through the window," Hagos says, nodding towards the tall window facing the garden. He quickly turns back to the staircase, and says out loud: "Stay back."

For a second, Marit thinks he's addressing the guy at the bottom of the steps, but then she realizes he's talking to her. From where Marit is, she can't see the guy, but she can hear him grunt and groan, and it sounds very much like he's making his way back up the stairs. Marit backs away as Hagos looks around the landing. The only thing there is a metal drying rack which her mom used to dry towels on. Right now, it's empty.

Hagos goes to the wall, and at first, Marit has no idea what he's doing. Then he reaches up and grabs the lamp that's mounted on the wall. It's one of her mom's favorites, and it cost a fortune, so Marit instinctively calls out for him not to break it, but he doesn't hear her. With one firm tug, he breaks the lamp free, and pulling hard, he rips the cord too. Then he strides back to the stairs just as the infected guy appears. He's walking in an uncertain manner—even more so than they all seem to do—and his head is lolling to one side, as though his neck is broken. This doesn't stop him from reaching out his arms to try and grab Hagos.

Hagos strikes the guy on the side of the head.

The lamp is made of steel or aluminum or some other metal, and it serves very effectively as a blunt instrument. The bulb shatters, but the rest of the lamp stays intact, as the infected guy goes flopping down the stairs for a second time.

Hagos stays poised, following him all the way down. A few seconds passes. Marit listens. A moan. A wet grunt. Then, sounds of someone coming up the steps again.

"God," Hagos mutters. "They just don't stop …"

Marit feels like peeing. She's afraid to go closer, but she's also afraid to go anywhere else, so she stays where she is, shifting her weight back and forth.

It takes the zombie longer to scale the stairs this time. Once he finally appears, Marit sees why: His leg is broken, and he's crawling. As soon as he reaches the drying rack, though, he grabs it and tries to push through.

Hagos leans forward and hammers the guy atop his head with the lamp. The zombie hisses, ducks, but then pops right back up. Hagos strikes him again, and again, like a gruesome game of whack-a-mole. Finally, after six or seven strikes with the lamp, the infected guy finally slumps over on his side and halfway rolls, halfway slides back down the steps.

CADAVER 4

Hagos drops the now blood-smeared lamp and steps back, breathing hard through his nose. He turns to look at Marit.

"Is he ... really dead?" she asks.

He nods.

Marit steps carefully closer. The guy has come to a halt around halfway down the stairs. He's lying in an awkward position, and his head looks like a lump of clay someone stepped on. The staircase is all covered in blood.

"Jesus, I'm never going down those steps again," Marit whispers.

"You'll have to," Hagos tells her. "Unless you want to stay here."

"I don't," she says, shivering. "I want to get as far away as I can."

"Good," Hagos says. "I found a car. That house over there, where I just was, there's an unlocked car. The keys—" He stops as his hand goes to his pocket. "Damnit! I must have left them. They were right there, on the kitchen counter."

Marit doesn't answer.

"Are you ready to leave?" he asks.

Marit wrinkles her nose and shakes her head. "I told you, I'm not going down those steps."

He sighs. "Is this your house?"

"Yes."

"That explains it."

"Explains what?"

"Next time, remember to close the front door after you."

"I did!" Marit says. "I closed it, and I locked it too!"

"No, you didn't," he says calmly, wiping sweat from his temple. "It was wide open."

"Well, then someone else must've opened it, because I sure as shit didn't leave the door open!" She feels angry with Hagos. Furious, actually. What makes him think he can talk to her like a parent talks to a kid? How dare he accuse her of being that careless? And in a situation like this? "I'm not stupid, you know. I know how to close a fucking door!"

He points over his shoulder. "Then how did *he* come in?"

"The hell should I know? He could have opened the door himself. Did you think of that?"

"They can't do that."

"Then ... then he must've been here already!"

"All right, calm down," he says, squinting as though her voice is giving him a migraine—which only makes Marit all the more angry. "At least the door is closed now—I slammed it as I came in." He looks around. "Do you have anything you want to bring? Extra clothes, maybe?"

Marit feels like slapping the guy—but he did just save her butt, so she makes an effort to calm down a little. And as she does, something hits her. "Wait ... did you say the front door?"

Hagos nods. "Yeah, why?"

"Because I came in through the terrace door." Marit shrugs. "That's the one *I'm* talking about."

Hagos frowns. "So ... the front door has been open all this time, while we were at the nursing home?"

Marit suddenly feels the anger being replaced by fear. "That's gotta be how he came in."

"Yes," Hagos says, his tone grim. "I just hope he's the only one who found his way into—"

As though reacting to a verbal cue, there comes a grunt from below. Both Hagos and Marit look down from the landing to see three infected people come into view from the far end of the kitchen.

"Oh, Jesus," Marit whispers, backing away. "Oh, no!"

Hago reacts quickly. He goes to the drying rack, grabs it, folds it up, then pins it down between the railings, effectively making a fence at the top of the stairs.

Marit doesn't think it'll hold them back. And as they reach the stairs and begin the ascent, she turns and runs to the room at the end of the hallway—her parents' bedroom.

"Wait!" Hagos calls after her. "Marit, stop!" He shouts something else, but Marit doesn't listen, and she doesn't stop, either.

At that moment, all she can think of is getting away from the three zombies about to come for them.

So, she runs into the bedroom, slams the door behind her and twists the key.

13

"I still think we should drive on," Belinda says.

Rosa looks at her, frowning. "But, Mom, what if they need help?"

"Yeah," Aksel agrees. "I say we at least have to find out." He drives closer to the guardrail, almost close enough that the bumper touches it. Leaning forward, he can see the bus's windscreen, which is facing the valley.

A pale face is staring out at him. It's a man, middle-aged, thin, large eyes. He's sitting on his ass, wearing what seems to be a uniform. It's hard to tell, because he's wrapped some kind of plastic around his torso, probably in an attempt to keep warm, and he's wearing a black beanie which makes him look like a burglar. His body looks oddly thick in comparison to his face, as though it's bloated slightly.

Aksel rolls down his window and calls out: "Hey there! You okay?"

"Please don't leave!" the man shouts, placing both hands on the window, his breath fogging up the glass. "Please! Please, don't go! I need help! I'm trapped in here! Please, I'm begging you!"

"Relax," Aksel tells him. "We're not leaving."

"Thank you," the man says, sounding almost on the verge of tears. He instead breaks into a shrill laughter. "Jesus, I thought I was in for. There's been three cars come by since we crashed, and all three of them just went right past. They saw me! I know they did, and they ... they just left anyway ..."

"It's a dog-eat-dog world," Aksel mutters. "More so now than before." Raising his voice, he says: "Is anyone else in there, or is it just you?"

"It's just me," the guy says, turning his head to glance towards the inside of the bus.

Aksel listens. The night is very quiet, and he picks up on low noises coming from the bus. Even though they're subtle, they're also unmistakable. Grunts. Groans. Scraping. Stumbling.

"Just you," Aksel says, "and how many infected people?"

The guy looks a little guilty, swallows, then says: "All right, look, there are a few of them. But, listen, listen!" He places his hands on the glass again, as though trying to keep them from driving away. "It's okay, really! They can't get to me. There's a metal grid, separating me from them. The cockpit …" He looks around quickly. "It's like a cage. It's reinforced on all sides. I'm trapped like a rat in here. I'll be dead by the end of the night if you guys don't help me. Please!"

"I don't like this," Belinda whispers. "If that bus is full of them, then this is very dangerous."

"They can't get out, either!" the guy shouts, as though hearing her. "Most of them are still in handcuffs. Some of them even died in the crash. Got their heads bashed in. I'm not lying, you can come see for yourself; there's no way they're getting to you. If you can just help me break this fucking glass so I can get out …"

"Are you a cop?" Anne asks, speaking suddenly.

"Uh-huh," the guy confirms, clumsily pulling the plastic aside to reveal his uniform. "Prison guard. I work up at Tromsø. They called us down here yesterday. I was driving this transport, I was bringing these infected people to a quarantine zone, when we crashed. It wasn't even my fault! Some guy came waddling out into the road. I think he might have been infected. I instinctively swerved to avoid him, but—" He shakes his head and shrugs. "Please, I have a daughter. Emma. She's only six years old."

"Where are the others?" Anne asks. "Your colleagues? Don't tell me you were transporting these people alone."

"No," the guy says, his voice breaking as he glances back at something not visible from where they're sitting. "My friend, Thormund, he, uhm … he didn't survive the crash. Broke his neck, I think."

"Sorry to hear it," Aksel says. "How long he's been dead?"

The guy's eyes flicker briefly, as though he's confused by the question. "He died … ten minutes after we crashed."

"And when was that?"

The cop shakes his head. "I don't … I don't know … Eight thirty, maybe …"

"So only a couple hours ago?"

"No, eight thirty this morning."

"Christ," Aksel mutters, looking around at the others. "Poor guy's been here all day. We need to help him out."

"If we do," Anne says in a low voice, "we'll also need to bring him along."

"We don't know him at all," Belinda interjects, leaning forward. "What if he's lying? What if he's infected?"

"Hey, buddy," Aksel calls. "You got any wounds?"

"No!" the guard shouts immediately. "No, I'm perfectly fine. Not a scratch."

"I'd love to take your word for it, but I hope you understand we need to be absolutely sure, so … would you mind stripping down?"

The guy scoffs. "Are you serious? It's like twenty below zero!"

"Yeah, we just need a quick look. You can keep your underpants on. Everything else needs to come off. That's our only demand. If you're clean, we'll help you bust that window and drive you to the nearest town."

Aksel expects Belinda to object to this, but she doesn't. Ever since the guy mentioned he has a daughter, Belinda's attitude seems to have shifted.

"Okay," the guy says, nodding. "Okay, I'll do it." He begins unwrapping the plastic.

Aksel opens the door.

"Where are you going?" Rosa asks.

"I need to check him up close. You guys stay here. I'll bring Guardian."

Aksel steps out and walks to the back. He opens the door and lets the dog out. He willingly jumps to the ground and shakes his fur.

"Come, boy."

The dog follows him willingly. As they approach the front of the bus, the guy is unzipping his pants. Aksel realizes the white stuff wasn't plastic at all, but fabric from the airbags. The guy seems to have cut them off after they got deployed in the crash, because stringy flaps are hanging from the dashboard.

Guardian gives a nervous whimper and hesitates.

"It's okay, buddy. They can't get to us. Come on."

The dog follows him, but it doesn't look happy about it. The hair on its back is standing on end, and it lowers its head.

The guard sees him coming and stops undressing to send him a pleading look. "Come on, man. Is this really necessary?"

"Sorry," Aksel says. "Nonnegotiable."

The guy huffs, but resumes undressing. He's already trembling all over, his nose is running, and his fingers are stiff and uncooperative, making it hard for him to unbutton the shirt. As he pulls it off, Aksel learns what made him look buff; he's wearing a second uniform.

Aksel steps close enough to look into the back of the bus. The guy wasn't lying about the grid. It's obviously meant to stop anyone from coming through, and it's working just fine. Four dead people are squeezing up against it, sticking their fingers through, snapping their teeth. They're wearing handcuffs, but regular civilian clothes. Aksel can only imagine how unnerving it must have been to spend several hours here, alone and scared, only four feet away from a flock of zombies wanting to eat you alive.

Looking past the hungry quartet, he sees at least a dozen others. Most of them are—just like the guard told them—still strapped in their seats, arms and legs dangling as they writhe to get free. On the floor—which is really the side—are maybe three or four who didn't survive the crash, their skulls either bashed in or clean missing.

"There," the guy says, pulling off his wife beater. "Happy?"

He's only wearing boxer briefs, socks and boots. He's even skinnier than Aksel thought, but also kind of ripped. He obviously spends time in the gym. His chest is smooth and hairless, and he's got a tattoo of some Chinese letters running down his ribs.

"Shoes too, I'm afraid."

"Oh, come on!"

"Dude, listen. If we find out you're hiding a missing toe, we'll have to shoot your brains out, okay? So do us all a favor and let me check."

The guy bends over and starts untying the laces. Aksel finally notices the other guy. He's been shoved into the corner, and he's been stripped down to his underwear. The way his head is turned, Aksel is pretty sure the guard was right in his diagnosis; poor guy broke his neck in the crash.

"Sorry about your partner," Aksel says. "At least he didn't come back. Were you guys close?"

"Just met him today," the guy says simply, yanking off his socks. "Okay, that's it. Are we good?"

"Turn around, please. Raise your arms."

The guard does as he's told, performing a shaky pirouette. Under any other circumstance, the situation would have been highly comical.

But Aksel doesn't feel like laughing at all. He leans in and studies the guy's skin.

"Okay, you look clean. Get dressed, and I'll—hey, you've got a gun?"

Aksel points at the handgun lying on a console next to the steering wheel. He didn't notice it until now because it's black like the rest of the dashboard.

"Yes, it's my service weapon," the guard says, quickly yanking his pants back on.

"Does it work?"

The guard sends him a strange look while putting his shirt on. "Of course. Why wouldn't it?"

"Couldn't you just shoot the windscreen?"

"I tried that," he says, pointing at the spot in the corner where there's a tiny star-shaped crack in the glass. "It's bulletproof. The projectile bounced right off, almost caught me in the face."

"Oh. Right." Aksel's plan was to use Anne's gun to shoot out the windscreen, but now he needs to rethink how they're going to get the guard out. He looks up. "And the door can't be opened?"

The guard pulls on his beanie and shakes his head. "At least not from the inside. It's open a crack, but I think the lock jammed when the bus tipped over."

"Lemme just try," Aksel says, stepping to the side to find a place to climb up. "Might be easier than breaking the windscreen."

"Careful," the guard warns him. "Don't go slipping now."

"Don't worry, I'm a decent climber." Aksel steps up onto the fender and scales the bus in a matter of seconds. Seeing the door, he immediately identifies the problem; it has suffered a blow, apparently from bouncing off the hillside, because there are traces of frozen dirt on it, and the metal has a large dent right above the handle. Unlike regular bus doors, this one actually has a handle. Aksel tries it, but the door is stuck. He squeezes his fingers through the crack and pulls hard. The hinges give off a low screech, and the door gives way a few millimeters.

"Is it working?" the guard calls from below.

"I think it can be done," Aksel says, wiping his nose. "Let me just get something."

He climbs back down and goes to the MPV. Guardian follows him. He opens the back door again, and the dog jumps in right away.

"Was he clean?" Belinda asks right away.

"Yeah, I think he's fine. We can't break the windscreen, but I think we can get the door open." He takes the red first-aid suitcase and opens it. Just as he hoped, there's a rolled-up nylon rope. He attaches one end to the MPV's towbar, then brings the other end over to the bus. He climbs back up and slips the rope inside. "Tie it to the door," Aksel instructs the guard. He jumps back down and goes back to the car.

As he gets back in behind the wheel, he rubs his hands together. Having spent only a few minutes outside, he's already shivering from cold.

"Sure that will work?" Belinda asks.

"Nope, not at all. But it's worth a shot. Here we go."

14

"Wait! Marit, stop! We don't know if there's more of them!"

Marit doesn't seem to hear him. Or if she does, she doesn't care. She reaches the door at the end of the hallway and slams it after her.

"Damnit," Hagos mutters, picking up the lamp as he backs away.

The fastest of the infected has already reached the top of the stairs. It's a young woman, around his own age, and she looks agile and athletic—she probably used to play handball, as a lot of young women do around here—but her playing days are clearly over, as evident by the fact that she's missing most of her thigh muscle and her right hand appears to have been gnawed off right above the wrist. It's now dangling from a couple of stubborn tendons like those strings you put in little kids' gloves to prevent them from dropping them in the snow.

The woman bumps into the drying rack and reaches for Hagos. He holds up the lamp, ready to strike, but the improvised fence holds her back, at least for now. But as she growls and pushes against it, it rattles and threatens to come free. The next infected person—a middle-aged man—joins her and increases the pressure on the drying rack.

It won't hold.

Hagos can't beat these three zombies like he did the first. For one thing, they're able to see. And there are too many hands groping for him now. In order to bash one of them over the head, he'd risk his hand getting scratched or grabbed.

So, he turns and runs after Marit.

He bumps into the door, surprised to find it locked. He taps the handle. "Marit? Let me in!"

No answer.

Has she jumped out the window?

He bangs the door hard.

"Marit? Come on, unlock the door!"

This time, Marit answers. She does so in a piercingly loud, terrified scream.

"Shit!"

Hagos looks back to see the drying rack topple over and the zombies come stumbling onto the landing.

He doesn't have time to try any of the other rooms. So, he steps back and throws himself at the locked door.

15

Not only does the trick with the rope work, it works even better than Aksel hoped.

He drives away from the bus very slowly, until he feels the rope getting taut. Then he increases the pressure on the accelerator slightly. Just as the engine revs up, there comes a snap from behind, and they lurch forward.

"Damnit, it broke," Aksel mutters, stopping the car.

"I don't think it did," Rosa says, looking out the rear window.

Aksel jumps out and finds that the girl is right. The rope is still intact. What gave way was the bus door, which is now standing upright on top of the bus. Through the windscreen, Aksel sees the guard, jumping and waving his arms, clearly exalted at the prospect of getting out.

Aksel runs over there and scales the bus once more. As he reaches the top, the guard has managed to climb up using the seats, and his head is sticking out. Aksel grabs his shoulders and hoists him up all the way.

"Oh, Jesus, oh, thank God," he mutters, clinging to Aksel while gulping in the icy night air. He's shivering all over, and his legs seem like they can't be trusted not to buckle at any moment. "Thank you, man," he mumbles, hugging Aksel tightly and slapping his back. "I owe you big time."

"Don't mention it," Aksel smiles. "You brought the gun?"

The guard's hand goes to his hip—where he's probably used to carrying his service weapon—and then he glances back down the opening. "Fuck. No, I left it."

"We need it." Already as he says it, he knows the guard isn't going back down there. As he's about to protest, Aksel goes on: "It's fine, I'll grab it. Can you climb down on your own, or do you need a hand?"

"I think I got it," the guard says, going to the edge and peering down. He turns and looks back. "Hey, I'm Folmer, by the way."

"Aksel. Be right back." He doesn't want to hang around out here in the freezing cold, so he quickly climbs down into the cockpit. The air is stuffier than he expected. A mixture of sweat, aftershave, and of course the infected people. And speaking of, as he turns towards to the grid, he's surprised to find that the deadly quartet has wandered off. They've all moved farther back, closer to where the MPV is parked, and are only now making their way back towards Aksel, stumbling and shoving through the bus.

This strikes him as odd, because until now, he's only ever seen the zombies go for the nearest prey, even if that prey was unreachable. And the guard—Folmer—was just inside the cockpit. He was definitely closer to them than the three women in the car.

They were probably drawn to the car because there are more people in it.

That seems like a logical explanation, and Aksel doesn't waste time wondering anymore about it. He turns to the gun on the tilted dashboard, and he can't help but glance at the corpse of the other guard. He seems to be already frozen stiff.

Really hope our plan will work. That once we get far enough north, even the undead will turn to ice.

Aksel grabs the gun and puts it down the back of his belt. As he goes to climb back up, he's met by three of the zombies who have reached the grid again and are all eagerly trying to get at him.

"Sorry, folks," he mutters, stepping up onto the seats. "No Aksel tartar today."

Climbing back out, he jumps down and runs to the MPV. Anne has come out to greet the guard, and Aksel is glad to see a little bit of life back in her eyes. She nods towards the backseat. "Hope you don't mind sitting close."

"Honestly, right now, I'd sit on a cactus if it was warm," the guard grunts, blowing into his frozen hands.

"What did you say your name was?"

"Folmer. Buddies call me Fozzy."

"Anne X. I'm with the force down in Trondheim."

Aksel notices the guard blink at this. "Oh. Fellow cop. Didn't expect that."

"Don't look so worried," Anne says, raising an eyebrow. "I'm not going to turn you in."

The guard nods with relief. "Thanks. Because I'm done with this crap. I'm going back home, and I'm staying there until they get this under control."

"Let's get inside," Aksel says, opening the door to the backseat.

The guard willingly climbs in, and Anne and Aksel return to the front seats.

"Call me Fozzy," the guard tells the women. "Hey, can we crank up that heater?"

"It's all the way up," Aksel says.

"Here," Rosa offers him the shirt she's been using.

"Thanks, darling," Folmer says. "Hey, why aren't you wearing any pants?"

"She lost them earlier," Belinda says, sounding defensive.

"Oh, all right. I just thought it was strange."

"I was caught in a situation kinda similar to yours," Rosa explains plainly. "Were you trapped in there for long?"

"All day," the guard mutters. "Longest day of my life."

"Can we please get going?" Belinda asks. "It's a little unnerving sitting here next to a bus full of infected people."

"Yeah," Aksel says, but he doesn't start driving. He instead looks from Anne to Folmer. "Don't you think we should call this in?"

"Why?" Folmer scoffs, as a violent shiver runs through him. "The infected folks aren't getting out. They're not a danger to anyone."

"No, but … you said you were on your way to a quarantine zone with them. Isn't someone waiting for you? Wondering where you are?"

"Yeah, you'd think so, wouldn't you?" Folmer sneers as he shakes his head. "Fucking assholes didn't even come looking for us. They knew the route. They knew we were supposed to be there by nine this morning. And where are they?" He looks over at the bus, and he shivers again. "The radio got busted in the crash, and I couldn't get a signal on my phone. But I figured, that's fine, they'll show up soon. Nah, they didn't. They just left me here to freeze to death. Because apparently, they don't give a fuck." He glances at Rosa, then at Belinda. "Sorry, but I'm pissed off. If it hadn't been for you guys, I'd be dead."

"I'm sure they're very busy today," Aksel says. "I'm not defending them, I'm just saying. By now, both the police and the army are involved, and they're probably stretched thin."

"Yeah, probably," Folmer concedes. "Could have sent someone to check, though."

"I think they just did."

Aksel looks at Anne. She's staring ahead. Following her gaze, he sees the road snake its way along the hillside. A quarter mile out are the headlights of something which can only really be a truck. And it's coming this way.

16

After turning the key, Marit goes straight to the windows.

Looking down, there's nothing but frozen lawn to break her fall. She already made a jump from this far up just a few hours ago, and her ankle throbs at the mere thought of doing it again. But there's no other way out of here.

"*Marit? Let me in!*"

She ignores Hagos. There's no way she's opening that door. Not with three zombies coming for them.

An idea occurs to her. She can use the duvets and the extra blankets in the closet as a landing pad. That way, she won't hurt herself. She grabs the duvets from the bed. As she strides across the floor, Hagos bangs hard on the door.

"*Marit? Come on, unlock the door!*"

Marit doesn't waste time answering. Instead, she throws the duvets out the window. Then she goes to the closet, pulls aside the sliding door, which is already ajar—and that's when she begins screaming. Stumbling back, her left foot, which isn't wearing a shoe, slips on the carpet, and she falls back, bumping against the soft bed.

Inside the closet, the old lady hisses and claws at Marit. She looks like she really wants to pounce on her, but she can't. Somehow, she's managed to get her left arm entangled in one of Marit's mom's summer dresses, the one with the drapes, and the straps are still clinging on to the coat hanger. But barely. And as the old woman lunges forward, the fabric begins to tear.

Marit is still screaming as the woman thrusts forward again. Surprisingly, the dress holds. So does the hanger. But the entire rod comes free, and all the coats, shirts, skirts and dresses come down. The woman doesn't pay any notice—she just crawls across the floor, clawing her way forward with her one free hand, while dragging along Marit's mom's entire wardrobe.

At that moment, there's a loud crash, and the door is suddenly flung open. Hagos comes bursting into the room, almost falling on his face.

It's enough to snap Marit out of it, and she jumps to her feet a split second before the woman can grab her. Marit runs around the bed, and the woman gets to her feet. Her right hand is finally freed, and she's able to stagger after Marit, effectively cornering her.

"No!" Marit shrieks. "Stay away!"

The woman doesn't hear her. She just keeps coming, reaching out her arms, as though wanting to embrace Marit. Marit can't get away. She can't do anything but scream.

Hagos runs up behind the old lady and shoves her hard in the back, causing her to stumble forward, lose her balance and slam into the wall only a few feet from where Marit is standing.

"Come on!" Hagos shouts, waving at her. "Let's go! Before she gets up!"

The old woman seems to be momentarily dizzy from bouncing her skull off the wall, and it takes her a few seconds to get her arms and legs to cooperate. She grunts, shakes her head and meticulously begins getting up.

"Come on, Marit! Now!"

Marit is about to run to Hagos. But then she sees them. Right behind him. Entering the room one at a time.

And she begins screaming again.

17

"What do we do?" Belinda asks from the backseat.

"There's nothing we *can* do," Anne says. "If that's the military—and I think it is—they'll want to hear what happened here."

"Fuck," Folmer hisses. "They can't identify me. They'll make me go back."

Aksel looks back. "Well, you're wearing your uniform, so there's probably no way around it."

The guard looks out the window, as though considering jumping out of the car and making a run for it. Then, to Aksel's surprise, he does exactly that, muttering, "Fuck it, there's no way I'm going back."

"Wait!"

But he's gone. Running around the car, he quickly scales the hillside and disappears into the darkness between the trees.

Next moment, the truck comes around the last part of the curve and into view. Even though the lights are blinding him, Aksel can tell immediately the truck really is military. At least he's never seen a regular truck looking this heavy duty.

"Are they ... are they going to arrest us?" Rosa whispers, as though the people in the truck can hear her.

"No, why would they?" Belinda asks.

Aksel glances at Anne. She doesn't say anything. She just looks at the truck. "What do you think?" he asks.

She doesn't look at him; she just shakes her head almost imperceptibly. "I have no idea. Let me talk to them."

Suddenly, a voice booms from what must be a loudspeaker, addressing them in accent-heavy English: "*Turn off the engine, please. Then step out of the vehicle. All of you.*"

"Goddamnit," Belinda hisses. "We should have just driven on."

"We would still have met them," Aksel mutters, shutting off the engine. "Let's just do as they ask, and—hey, what are you doing?"

Anne takes out her gun, and for a terrifying moment, Aksel thinks she's going to open fire at the truck, effectively turning them into a shooting tent. Instead, she opens the door, steps out, and places the gun on the roof of the MPV. "Anne X," she shouts, showing her badge. "Constable from Trøndelag Police District."

After a brief pause, the voice comes again, this time in Norwegian: "*Hello, Constable. Who's with you?*"

"Three civilians," Anne says. "A young man, a young mother and a little girl." She glances back. "We also have … a large dog."

"*Any more weapons in the car?*"

"No."

"*Could you please tell them to exit the vehicle? The dog stays.*"

Anne looks in at them. Aksel has already unbuckled. Stepping back out into the freezing air, he raises his hand against the blinding light in a brief greeting gesture. Rosa and Belinda come out too, squinting and holding each other.

"*Are any of you infected?*"

"No," Anne says firmly.

"*What are you doing here?*"

"We were just passing. We had to slow down in order to edge by the bus."

"*Have you been in contact with anybody inside the bus?*"

Anne hesitates only briefly at this. "No. We had a quick look. When we found no one alive, we decided to drive on. We were just about to when you showed up."

Another pause. Then the lights are switched to a much less intense level, and Aksel can make out the soldiers stepping out onto the pavement. They're dressed in what looks like full winter uniforms, complete with white helmets, ski glasses and neck gaiters covering everything below the eyes. They carry proper military rifles as well, and Aksel feels immediately tense. Last time he saw soldiers up close was back at the containment zone outside the hospital.

He still isn't sure if they'd managed to figure out his identity after he escaped. If they did, there could be a warrant out for him. If these soldiers find out who he is, they'll probably arrest him again.

Three times within two days, Aksel thinks grimly. *That's gotta be a new record.*

His mind runs over things that could give him away. He hasn't got his wallet on him, and nothing else with his name. His phone is in his pocket, but he could smash it before they took it. Other than that, there's really only two things: his prints, which he knows are in the system, because he got pulled over a few years ago while riding his dirt bike in the hills outside of town, which turned out to not meet the sound restriction laws due to a faulty muffler, or some of the others telling on him. He can't see why they would do that, though.

One of the soldiers comes to them, while two others go to the bus. They approach it carefully, keeping their weapons ready, using the flashlights mounted on the barrels. It's surreal to Aksel, seeing a scene like this, which he's only ever watched in movies. They begin checking all around the bus. "Infected people inside," one of them shouts as soon as he gets a look through the windscreen. "At least a dozen."

"Can they get out?" the soldier in front of them asks.

"Doesn't look like it."

"No, they would have probably left already," the soldier mutters, looking at Anne. He's placed his glasses on his forehead, but his mouth is still covered. "What are you doing all the way up here, Constable?"

Aksel knew the question would come, but he has no idea what Anne is going to answer. She told them she would do the talking, and he trusts her.

"I'm taking these people to safety," she says simply. "We're going farther north, outside the reach of the infection."

The soldier raises an eyebrow. "I've got depressing news, Constable. In a matter of days, there won't be such a thing as 'outside the reach of' this thing. Not unless you find a rocket ship." He nods towards the bus. "We're doing our best, but things like this keep happening. We've been running nothing but damage control since we were called up here, but we can't keep up. Who knows how many infected people wandered off this crash site? We'll never be able to track them down before they infect others."

"How far has it spread now?"

He shrugs. "They say it's already in Sweden."

One of the other soldiers comes back. "We count fourteen, Sergeant. Four are moving freely. None of them can get out."

The sergeant nods. "All right. Get them secured. Begin with those four free-roamers." As the soldier runs back to the truck, the sergeant sighs and rubs his eyes with his gloved hand. "If we could just put a bullet in them, then maybe we'd have a fighting chance."

"Why don't you do that?" Aksel asks, speaking before he can think. He didn't want to draw attention to himself, but the question just slips out.

The soldier looks at him. "Because we're human beings, and as far as we know, so are they."

Aksel nods, but thinks to himself: *Well, you're wrong.*

"Has there been any success in curing them?" Anne asks, deftly shifting the focus back to herself.

"Not from what I've heard, no. Between you and me ..." He lowers his voice, and Aksel has to strain to hear him over the rumble of the truck's engine. "There won't be any cure. I don't know if they can find a vaccine like they did with Covid, but I'm telling you, soon as this infection is in your blood, you're done for. I've seen it a ton of times. One little scratch, fever, then ..." He glances towards the bus. "There's no coming back from that final stage."

"I agree," Anne says. "When you see them up close, they look almost dead."

The soldier scoffs. "They don't *look* dead, Constable. I've seen my share of dead people. I know what human eyes look like when the lights have gone out. And those poor infected people ... they're not really here no more. I'm sure of it. It's like that awful infection is keeping them going, like string puppets or something. They're sure not doing it on their own."

"Then how can you call them humans?" Belinda asks. Whether it's because her tone is friendlier than Aksel's, or due to the fact that she's a woman, Aksel doesn't know, but the soldier doesn't hard-eye her as much. "I mean, if they're basically walking corpses ... Wouldn't the merciful thing be to put them down?"

The soldier doesn't answer right away. Over by the bus, the two other soldiers have pulled out what to Aksel looks almost like equipment a dog catcher would use: net, muzzles and catch poles with wire nooses at the end.

"That your daughter?" the soldier asks.

"Yes," Belinda says, pulling Rosa in tighter.

"If she got infected and reached the last stage, would you want her taken to a place where they'd try to cure her—even if you knew they likely wouldn't succeed—or would you have her put down on the spot like a rabid dog?"

Belinda squeezes her lips together.

"I thought so," the soldier mutters. "Even dead people still have families who love them." He looks at Anne. "So, why are you not on duty, Constable?"

"I was," she says right away. "But I got relieved."

"Relieved? Under these circumstances? You must have won the lottery."

It's obvious he doesn't believe her. It's just as obvious that Anne isn't rattled the slightest by this. She says plainly: "My entire division was scattered and killed. Last thing my boss told me was to hunker down at my location, because I was the only one left within miles, and the entire city was being overrun by infected people. Help never came, so I had to break out of there. I was going to get my daughter, when I learned she's dead."

"Oh," the soldier says. "My, uhm, condolences."

None of them seem to know what to say next.

One of the other soldiers comes by, handing the sergeant what looks a lot like those laser thermometers they used at the roof of the hospital.

The sergeant clears his throat. "I'm afraid I'll need to check your temperatures. It's protocol. The three Fs and all that."

"Three Fs?" Aksel asks.

The sergeant places his rifle on his back and looks from Aksel to Anne. "You haven't heard? *Feber*, *farve* and *flenger*? Two out of three, and we gotta bring you in."

Aksel almost bursts into laughter. That's so typical of the government. Taking something this gruesome and turning it into a matter of three simple symptoms that are easy to remember and even a child could understand. He doesn't even need any explanation to know what the soldier will look for in them. Feber means fever, farve is color, which must refer to discoloration of the skin, and flenger is also self-evident; it means scratches.

The sergeant proceeds to scan them all with the laser. All of them check out okay. Except Belinda.

"Huh," the sergeant says, eyeing her. "One-oh-one. That's a fever. You've been in contact with anyone infected?"

"Well, no, but—"

"But what?" the sergeant asks, taking a step back. "You were in contact with anyone or not?"

"I didn't touch anyone," Belinda says, shaking her head, "and I certainly wasn't bitten or scratched. The fever must be because of my mono. It's acting up."

The sergeant doesn't look convinced. "All right. I'll have to check you for fresh wounds now, and you understand if I find any, I have no choice but to bring you in, right?"

"Oh, Jesus," Belinda mutters.

"What?" Aksel asks, confused. "You have any wounds?"

He never saw Belinda get close enough to any of the zombies to have sustained a scratch or a bite. And even if she did, wouldn't she have turned by now? Then again, he couldn't know for sure how long it took. Had she been hiding a wound this entire time? Was the mono just a clever excuse so they wouldn't question it when she began spiking a fever?

"What?" the sergeant asks sharply, drawing back farther. "You have any wounds?"

"Listen, please," Belinda says. "I'm not infected, okay? I told you, it's mono."

"Kim!" the sergeant shouts. "I think we have one here."

"No!" Belinda shouts, hugging Rosa, who in return is clinging to her. "I'm not infected! I'm not! I swear, I never touched any of them!"

Aksel doesn't know what to say or do, so he simply stands there, staring at Belinda, trying hard to read her. Has she been playing them this entire time? Placing all of them in danger, including her own daughter? He can't believe that. But the simple fact is, he doesn't know her well enough. He also doesn't know what it's like having to care for your daughter. Wouldn't you do anything to stick around for as long as possible?

The sergeant pulls out a handgun. He doesn't take aim at Belinda, but he holds it ready. "I need you to show me your wound. The rest of you, step aside, please."

One of the other soldiers has joined them, standing off to the side. He seems to have caught on right away that Belinda is the one in question, and he's blocking her from running.

Anne obeys, taking a few steps away. Aksel finds himself moving back, too. Rosa doesn't let go of her mother.

"Please," Belinda says, sounding like she's about to cry. "You can run a blood test. Or just ... just look it up in my medical journal! That's available online, right? It'll tell you I was diagnosed two years ago."

"Even if I could do that, which I can't, only doctors can, that still wouldn't prove anything. And it also wouldn't change my orders."

"Please, you have to understand—"

"No!" the sergeant cuts her off, raising his voice and pointing at her with the gloved hand not holding the gun. "*You* need to understand, lady. I'm not here to do a medical checkup or to diagnose you. My only job is to determine whether you go or come with us. Now, unless you voluntarily show me where you're hurt, I'm gonna have to get Kim here to secure you, then strip you down. I really don't think you'd want that."

Belinda drops her head and begins weeping.

Rosa looks up at her, fear, confusion and concern painting on her face. "Mom?" she asks. "Is it true? Are you ...?"

Belinda pulls herself free from her daughter, then pushes her away. It seems to require all her willpower, and she starts crying even harder. Then she takes a stern breath and looks Rosa in the eye. "It'll be okay, honey. I promise. I'm not infected. I swear to you. But they won't believe me."

"Oh, no," Rosa says, shaking her head. "No, Mom ..."

She steps forward again, but Belinda holds up her hand. "No," she says firmly. "Stay back, sweetie. Or they'll just take you too."

"Jesus Christ," Aksel hears himself breathe.

"Last chance," the sergeant tells Belinda. "Show us, or we're stripping you down."

Belinda hesitates for another moment. They're all just staring at her. Then, as the sergeant is about to step forward, Belinda looks right into Aksel's eyes and says quietly, "It was the wire. I swear it."

He has no idea what she means.

But then she bends down and pulls up her pant leg. Across her calf runs a nasty, bright-pink scratch. Aksel has seen enough burn wounds from ropes to recognize right away that this is not a scratch from a nail or anything else pointy. The skin isn't sliced; it's torn open due to friction. It falls into place for him, then. How Belinda must have slit her leg across the wire when she climbed across the parking lot, probably multiple times. It's easy to hurt yourself when you aren't used to that kind of acrobatics.

Rosa starts crying.

Belinda pleads with the soldiers, tells them again and again it's not what they think, begs them to believe her.

The sergeant says he has no choice.

Neither Anne nor Aksel says or does anything; they both know it's pointless.

In a matter of seconds, Belinda is in handcuffs, and even though her hands are already behind her back, they also strap what looks like heavy-duty winter mittens on her.

As the sergeant leads her towards the truck, Rosa runs for her, but Aksel steps in and grabs her. "Don't," he says in her ear. "If you touch her again, they might take you as well."

"It'll be all right," Belinda says, sounding like she's desperately trying to believe that herself. "Once they see I'm not getting worse, I'll be allowed to go, right? Right?"

She stares at the sergeant as he takes her around to the back of the truck. Aksel and Rosa follow along at a safe distance, Aksel holding firmly onto the girl's shoulders.

"That's not up to me," the sergeant says regrettably.

One of the other soldiers unlocks the back door and swings it open.

"Step up, please," the sergeant says, gesturing to the bumper step.

"But they won't keep me there when I'm not infected, right?" Belinda asks, not moving.

The sergeant sighs. "I just don't know. All I can say is, since you're obviously not last stage, you'll be put in with the SIs—'suspected infected.'"

Aksel immediately feels his stomach tighten as he recalls the containment outside the hospital in which he, Linus and several other people were kept. All of them were suspected infected, and those who weren't *actually* infected stood a pretty slim chance of getting out alive.

"Wait," Belinda begins, but the sergeant halfway pushes, halfway hoists her up into the truck.

"Mom!"

"Where are you taking her?" Aksel asks.

The sergeant stops at the step and sends a hard look over his shoulder. "To a secure facility." His eyes land on Rosa, and his expression softens somewhat. "Look," he says, addressing Anne. "I can't tell you where it is. And I advise you strongly not to follow us. They take security extremely seriously. Anyone spotted in the vicinity will be arrested and end up inside."

With these words, the sergeant turns and pushes Belinda inside the truck. Aksel peers inside to see two rows of seats—and to his horror, he sees three of them are already taken. Two zombies and one very-soon-to-be have been strapped in. The two undeads immediately stretch their necks for Belinda—or at least they try to. They're all wearing muzzles, and these are attached to the wall behind them with short straps, making them only able to move their heads a few inches. The person who hasn't turned yet, but obviously soon will, is an old, skinny guy wearing a heavy hunting coat. In the dim light from small red lamps in the ceiling, Aksel can tell the guy is visibly sweating. His mouth is hanging open, and saliva is dripping from the muzzle grid. He's missing a shoe, and also, apparently, a couple of toes. Someone, which could be the guy himself, tried to wrap up the wound with something that looks like duct tape. While the makeshift bandage has managed to stem the blood flow, it can't hide the fact that the rest of the guy's foot is all green.

"Oh, God," Rosa exclaims as she sees the zombies. "You can't put her in there with them!"

The sergeant doesn't answer. He places Belinda all the way at the back, across from the two zombies, and one seat away from the comatose guy. He shoves her down, gently but firmly, and locks the belts around her thighs and chest. Then, before he straps on the muzzle, Aksel hears him mutter: "Sorry about this. I'm afraid there's no way around it."

Once the muzzle is secured the sergeant steps back.

Belinda turns her head and looks out at them. She reminds Aksel of Hannibal Lecter. Her eyes are huge and terrified, and the fact that she tries to smile just makes it worse. "It'll be all right, sweetie. I promise. Once they let me go, I'll call you, and we'll find each other. Okay?"

"O-okay," Rosa says shakily. "I love you, Mom."

Belinda bursts into tears. "Love you too, sweetie. See you soon!"

Then the view is cut as the sergeant comes back out and gestures for them to move back. They step aside as the other soldiers begin bringing over the zombies from the bus. Using the catch poles, they're able to handle one zombie each, which is quite effective. In a matter of minutes, they have guided all the infected into the truck and secured them.

Then they simply get in, turn the vehicle around, and drive back the way they came, leaving Anne, Aksel and Rosa next to the bus in the quiet, freezing night.

18

He spins around to see what Marit sees—even though he already knows. He just hoped he had a few more seconds. But the three infected people managed to push through the drying rack and are now all entering the bedroom, which despite its impressive size suddenly feels very, very small.

The sporty woman is still in front, and she heads straight for Hagos. He turns back and intends to grab Marit. They have no other choice than to jump across the bed and head for the window, and if they're quick, it can still be—

Hagos freezes for a brief instant as he can't see Marit anywhere. The girl has stopped screaming and moved away from the corner. She's now crawling across the bed, and as though she's read his mind, she seems to be headed right for the window. The old lady tries briefly to reach her, but scaling the tall bed seems too much trouble for her, so she instead turns to come for Hagos.

The young handball player growls right behind him, and as Hagos jumps forward, he feels her fingers graze the back of his shirt, almost catching him. He runs right at the old woman. He has no other choice than to push her over once more, and this time he doesn't have the advantage of coming up from behind. Instead, he shoves her hard in the chest, then immediately retracts his arms. Even with how fast he does it, she still manages to grab for him, and her long nails run all the way down his arms. Had he worn short sleeves, he would have no doubt been scratched bloody.

The woman slams against the wall again, this time it's the back of her head that takes the brunt of it, and Hagos can hear her teeth chatter as she flops to the ground. It gives him a second to jump onto the bed. Marit has already climbed up onto the windowsill, but she's hesitating and looking back at him. The sporty woman immediately leans over the bed and grabs for him, and one of the other infected has staggered around to the other side of the bed, cutting off Hagos from reaching Marit and the window.

"Damnit!" he hisses, stepping back as the woman almost reaches him. She climbs onto the bed, snarling eagerly. "Go, Marit!" he shouts. "Just jump!"

He doesn't wait and see if she does it or not, because the infected guy now comes for him from the other side, and he has no choice left but to run to the foot of the bed and jump down. As he does, the third infected guy swoops in from the side and grabs hold of his upper arm. Hagos wrenches free and catches the guy with an elbow right under the chin, causing him to stagger back a few steps.

Looking back, he sees Marit still sitting in the window, still looking back. She isn't in any particular rush, because the window is all the way across the room, and Hagos is much closer to the infected people, meaning that all three of them are coming for him. He backs up against the closet, and without much thought, he slips inside and pulls the sliding door closed less than half a second before the zombies reach it.

19

"Let's get in the car," Anne suggests in a low voice. "Before we freeze to death."

Aksel brings Rosa along, his arm around her shoulders, and they take the backseat together. Anne gets in behind the wheel and turns on the engine.

Guardian whimpers from the back. Aksel isn't sure how much the dog understands of what just went down, but as he glances back to see its large, somber eyes, he gets the clear feeling the big guy is very much aware that they just lost a member of their group. It stretches its thick neck to sniff Rosa's hair and lick her ear.

Rosa stops crying and offers him her hand, which Guardian immediate starts rubbing his snout against. Her tiny, pink fingers look even smaller next to the dog's giant mouth, which could bite them off as easy as a hacksaw could cut a tuft of grass. The dog's only intention, though, is to comfort the girl, and it seems to work. In half a minute or, Rosa seems to feel better.

"Do you really think they'll let her go again?" she asks, addressing both Aksel and Anne. "When they find out she's not infected? I mean, will they just be like, 'sorry for the inconvenience, here's your phone, let us call you a cab.' I just … I just don't think it's realistic."

Aksel is once again struck by the way the young girl talks. It's not only that she's clearly older than her age, it's also how she's cutting to the chase and being completely honest.

"I don't know," Anne mutters, shaking her head. "I just don't. Under normal circumstances, I would trust the authorities. But these aren't normal circumstances by any stretch."

"Based on what went down in Torik," Aksel says, "I'm not too hopeful. I also think there's a big risk that she'll … become infected by staying at wherever they're taking her. I mean, there are probably hundreds if not thousands of zombies there."

Rosa looks very uncomfortable at the thought. "But he said they'll keep her separated from them."

Aksel shrugs. "Back at the hospital, where they kept me and Linus along with a bunch of other people, someone would turn every few minutes, and the rest of us would be at great risk. It was like being locked in with predators that could wake up any moment, and there was nowhere to run; we just had to rely on the soldiers acting fast enough whenever someone passed out." Taking himself back there in his mind, he can't help but feel his chest start to constrict. "But of course, they might run a tighter operation here. I just don't think it likely they have the resources to keep every single person separate."

Rosa was watching him while he talked. Now, she lowers her gaze and nods, accepting what he said as probably true. "So … even if she survives and is allowed to go, they probably won't let her call me like she said she would. I mean, if the location is confidential like he said. And they probably won't waste time driving her anywhere, either."

"No," Aksel says grimly. "I think it's more likely they'll keep her phone and show her the door."

Rosa takes a deep, steadying breath. "So, what do we do now? We can't just wait around, hoping to hear from my mom. I guess we either drive on, or we go looking for her. Those are our two options, right?"

Again, Aksel is struck by how bluntly the girl is analyzing the situation and stating the facts of it.

"Basically, yeah," Anne says. "And even if we could find her, we'd have to break in to get her out."

"Do we have any ideas as to where she might be?" Aksel asks, looking at Anne.

She shrugs. "I'm not very familiar with the area. I assume they chose a location away from any major towns. Perhaps they used an industrial complex or something—I know there are large factories up here, but I have no idea where to start looking."

A moment of silence in the car. Guardian is breathing audibly. Aksel chews the inside of his cheek. "If we do this," he says, looking at Rosa. "If we go looking for your mom, there's one thing we need to get out of the way first."

The girl just looks back at him, waiting.

He's not sure how to phrase the question, so he simply puts it out there: "The mono ... that was real. Right?"

A slight crease on Rosa's forehead. "Are you suggesting she used it to cover up the fact that she was infected?"

Aksel feels the blood rush to his face. "I'm just saying ... we need to rule that out."

Rosa looks at him a little longer. Then she nods. "She really does have mono."

"And you don't think she could possibly have used it as an excuse?" He quickly adds: "People will do insane things when they know they're dying."

Rosa shakes her head. "My mom isn't the bravest person, but she would never place me in danger." That's all she says. She then resumes petting Guardian, as though the matter has been sufficiently dealt with. No emotions. No raised voice or angry remarks like, "how dare you?" or "do you think you know my mom better than me?" Not even a sour look. Rosa took Aksel's words for exactly what they were: a necessary question to rule out.

Damnit, I like her. If everyone's brains worked like hers, there'd be much less drama in the world.

Anne seems about to say something, when Guardian suddenly whips his head to the side and starts growling.

Aksel looks in the direction of his gaze, and he sees a figure coming out from the trees. It's clearly not a dead person, because the guy is running without stumbling, headed right for the car.

"Look who's back," Anne says with a slightly snarky tone.

The guard grabs the passenger door. When it doesn't open, he rapidly taps the window. "Hey, please let me in! I'm freezing!"

Anne turns in her seat to look back. She looks even more tired and worn than usual. "We have no choice, right?"

Aksel shakes his head. "No, we can't leave him."

Anne hits the central lock, and the door snaps. The guard gets in, holding himself, shivering violently. "Christ, I thought for sure I was gonna lose a limb out there. Hey, thank you folks for waiting for me."

Aksel had pretty much forgotten about the guard, but he doesn't say that. Instead, he says, "They took Belinda."

"Oh," the guard says, looking back. "Jeez, I didn't even notice. Why did they ...? Was she infected?"

"No," Aksel says. "She had a completely unrelated virus which was causing a slight fever. They just didn't believe her."

"Oh, right," the guard says, looking like he doesn't buy it, either. "Well, we're instructed not to take any chances, so ..."

"We?" Anne asks. "Where exactly were you taking the people on the bus?"

"To the quarantine zone," the guard says, as though that was obvious.

"Is that where they took my mom?" Rosa exclaims.

The guard looks back at her, then at Anne once more. "I would assume so, yeah. Why?"

A moment of silence in the car, as they all exchange looks.

"Because we're going to get her," Aksel says finally.

"Hey, no, wait a second," the guard says, holding up his hands, like a soccer player who just tackled someone and denies having anything to do with it. "I don't know what you think, but that place is not a nursing home. You can't just drop in for a visit and ask to bring someone home."

"We'll deal with that when we get there," Aksel says. "What's the address?"

"Look, you don't get it. I'm not going back there. Not a chance."

"Well, it's either that," Anne says in an even tone, giving him a dead-eye stare. "Or you're not going anywhere. At least not in this car."

20

She can do nothing but stare as the three zombies close in on Hagos, then, just a moment before they reach him, he slips inside the closet and closes the door.

The infected immediately begin clawing away at the surface. Even though the door was closed right in front of them, they apparently have no idea how to open it again. None of them even try to push it sideways. Instead, they use their nails and teeth, trying to dig their way through the obstacle. It's made of solid wood, and it will take them hours.

A few moments pass. Nothing but the grunts and snarls from the zombies are heard.

Despite the fact that Marit is literally a sitting duck, the infected people aren't coming for her. They must know she's there, because they've all seen her. But they not so much as turn around to glance at her. They seem much more eager to get at Hagos. It must be because he's a lot closer—practically inches away—but he's also protected by the closet door.

"Marit?" he suddenly calls out for her, causing her to jump. "You still here?"

"Y… yes," she says, clearing her throat. She's afraid to talk, as it might draw the zombies.

But they don't react to her voice at all. They just resume what they're doing.

"You need to help me."

"How would I do that?"

"If you lure them away for just a couple of seconds, I can make a run for the door."

"But ... that would put me in danger."

"You only need to take a few steps closer. As soon as they come for you, you run back and jump out the window."

"I can't ... I can't do that."

"Yes, you can. You have to."

"No, I'm sorry."

"Listen, if you don't, then I'll never get out of here. The house is locked, and no one might come for days. I'll die of thirst."

He says it in a pretty even tone, as though he's trying not to freak out.

"I'm sure you'll be fine," Marit says. "I'm sure someone will come for you." She feels a little bad for leaving him, but as soon as he stepped into the closet, she knew it wasn't going to end well for him. She was never going to risk her own life for him. Not even if he begins pleading.

Which he doesn't. Instead, he keeps his voice calm as he says: "Marit, I hate to say this, but I helped you out more than once."

"I know, and that ... that was totally your choice. And this is mine." She shrugs, as though Hagos can see her. "I'm not fast and strong like you. And I have a bad ankle. I might trip or something. I'm sorry, but there's just no way I'm taking that risk."

"Marit, at least try to—"

"I'll tell the police where you are. I promise."

She turns around to face the fall and the pile of duvets below. It's not much, not as much as she'd like, but they should act as a cushion.

"Marit? ... *Marit?!*"

She doesn't answer. She breathes in a mouthful of the cold air, steadies herself, then, letting out a tiny shriek, she pushes off the windowsill.

21

"You guys are crazy," the guard mutters, chowing down potato chips by the fistful. "You're getting us all detained."

None of them bother to answer. They've been driving for half an hour, and the guard has made similar remarks every few minutes. Aksel knows he's right, of course. Going to fetch Anne from a highly secured containment facility is next-level stupid, and it just might end badly. But he also knows there's no other choice. They at the very least have to give it a try. Because of Rosa.

"What's the address?" Anne asks, glancing at the guard.

"I told you, it's closed and has been for years. It doesn't have an address!"

"Coordinates, then?"

"How should I know?" he grunts. "Do I look like a GPS?"

Anne looks like she's about to tell him exactly what he looks like, so Aksel jumps in: "Tell us about the place, then. You said it's an abandoned prison?"

"Yeah, that's pretty much all I know. It was closed down sometime in the eighties, I think. Lack of space, probably. But the buildings up there are still fine, and really, an empty correction facility located in the middle of nowhere is a pretty ideal place to put a bunch of highly dangerous and contagious people, right? I think for once, some of the higher ups made the right call."

Aksel isn't too sure about that. Isolating the infected might seem like a good idea, but it also meant placing them all in the same place, basically creating a horde. If anything went wrong and they somehow overran the place, several thousand zombies in one huge group would be all but impossible to stop. Facing them one or two at a time, even a dozen or so, that was doable, provided you had the weapons or enough space around you to run away. But an undead army ... that could lay waste to an entire city, even one as big as Oslo.

"I'm finally warming up," the guard says, taking off the second uniform. "I never thought my blood would get going again."

"Fostervoll," Anne mutters, reading his name from his shirt tag. "That's you?"

"Uh-huh."

Anne stares at him for a moment, and the guard seems to become unnerved by it.

"What? Do we know each other?"

"No," Anne says, shaking her head and looking back out at the road. "I just ... your name rang a bell, that's all."

"Well, it's a small country," the guard says. "And my family name is pretty unique."

"It is." Anne appears to want to say something else, but she changes her mind, and simply repeats: "It is."

They drive on for a few minutes.

"Okay," the guard says, "in about two hundred meters, there's a fork in the road. Take the right."

Anne gives a nod of confirmation.

"We're getting close," the guard goes on, looking out his window. "In a couple of minutes, we should see the lights."

Rosa leans forward. "Thank you for doing this."

The guard looks back in surprise. "Well, I'm, uh ... it's not like I have a choice," he grunts. "But you're welcome."

"Still, I'm grateful," Rosa says. "If not for you, I might never have seen my mom again. This way, I at least get the chance."

Keeping expectations low, Aksel thinks. *Clever girl.*

"Yeah, well, I hope you find her," the guard says, smiling awkwardly before turning back around.

"You said you had a daughter?" Rosa goes on.

"Yeah, can't wait to see her. My little Anna."

Aksel frowns. "Anna? Thought you said her name was Emma."

The guard looks back a little too quickly. "I did? Must have been a slip of the tongue."

He stiffly looks ahead again.

Anne sends Aksel a look. She picked up on the obvious lie as well.

"You don't get your kid's name wrong," she scoffs. "He's not a parent at all."

The guard sends her a sour look. "Okay, so what? What difference does it make?"

"It makes a big difference. You lied. You manipulated us."

He throws out his hands. "I just said what you wanted to hear. You were still debating whether to help me or not. You're the real hypocrite!"

"Oh, really?"

"Yeah, really. It shouldn't make a difference if someone has a kid or not. So what if I'm not a parent? That mean I'm not worthy of saving? What kind of sick discrimination is that?"

No one answers him. They reach the fork in the road, and Anne makes a right. They drive on for a little while in silence.

"Look, I get it," Aksel says. "You told a white lie in order to make sure we would help you. It wasn't necessary, though; we would have gotten you out regardless. But ..."

"But what?"

"But now I'm worried we can't trust you. That you're taking us somewhere else."

The guard grunts. "If you need proof, look over there." He points, and Aksel follows his finger.

Across the valley, he sees a scattering of lights on the side of the hill. It could be a tiny village, except the lights are orange and placed in a specific pattern.

"That's the place," the guard says, glancing back at Rosa. "That's where your mom is."

22

"Marit?"

He listens over the groans and scratching and fumbling. No answer from the girl.

"*Marit*?!"

He hears a brief squeal, but that's all.

Holding the closet door in place—not that he really needs to, they haven't even tried to slide it aside yet, but he doesn't want to take the chance—he frowns in the darkness.

Did she just jump out?

He decides not to call for her again. It's no use either way; he can't change her mind. She's either coming back to help him, or she's leaving. It's out of his control. He said all he could.

Well, that's not true. He could have begged her. Except he won't do that. He's got too much pride, which is probably his biggest flaw. Hubris doesn't jive with survival. He thought he would do anything to save his life, but apparently, there's a limit.

Probably wouldn't have worked anyway, he thinks, running his sleeve across his forehead. It comes away damp. Not good. Means he'll get thirsty soon. But even with the window wide open—as he assumes it still is—the closet is stifling.

After a few minutes or so with no more noises from Marit, he decides she probably did jump.

She might still come back. Maybe she's looking for someone who can help. She could be bringing back a police officer.

But Hagos can't convince himself of any of that. What he saw before coming here didn't look promising at all. He doesn't think for a second the authorities have the situation under control, nor will they get it anytime soon.

And Marit isn't coming back. She's only focused on saving her own ass. He knew the moment he met her that she was not a brave soul, not someone to risk her own life for someone else. Especially not someone she doesn't know. Still, he feels a red-hot anger fire up inside. She likely left him for dead. And all because she's a coward who wouldn't even try to help him, even though he—

Hagos closes his eyes firmly and willfully disentangles his mind from the hateful thoughts. True as they may be, he can't engage in them. Not now. He's been down that path countless times. He knows where it ends. Knows it intimately. Anger, resentment, regret, they all lead to the same place. A place of confusion, of desperation.

What he needs is a clear head. Concise action. And he needs it now more than ever. With everything he's been through, this might be the most dangerous situation he's ever faced. But it's no different, really. The stakes are just raised slightly. Which means he needs to raise his game, too.

He takes several deep inbreaths, helping the air all the way down to his belly, ignoring the constant, invasive noises from the three infected people right on the other side of the door. It works. Narrowing his focus down to his breathing, he manages to loosen up the crackling fireball of anger in his solar plexus. He feels it release into his body as energy before it dissipates.

After a few more minutes, he feels calm inside. Empty of thought and emotion. He's back in the control room, and he's got freedom of choice.

Right. Options. What are they?

Limited, that's for sure. For one thing, he left his phone in his car. He always did so, because he never used it during his shifts. So calling anyone for help is out—which probably wouldn't have saved him anyway. He's sure the police are still busy. Back at Edith's apartment, they tried calling them and only got reassured they were already doing everything they could.

And Hagos only has one friend here in town. Juma. Who's exactly not the type of person you'd call in a situation like this. Even if Juma hadn't left town yet, and even if Hagos could convince him to come, guiding him on the phone, he's not really sure Juma could do the job of luring he infected people away without either panicking or getting himself bitten.

But it's useless wondering, because Hagos doesn't have his phone, so he can't call anyone. Whatever needs to happen, it'll be up to him alone.

He looks around. The closet has its back against the wall, and it goes all the way to the ceiling. Meaning, there's no getting out through the back, the top, or the floor; the only way is through the door.

Or rather, *doors*. Plural.

He noticed the closet had two doors, of which he chose the right, because it was already open. Looking to the side, his eyes have tuned into the darkness just enough by now that he can make out the dividing wall separating the two halves of the closet. He assumes that since this side had coats and dresses, the other probably has shelves. He knocks on the wall. It's made of wood, but it's not terribly thick. He could probably break it down with his hands.

Would getting access to the other side of the closet really do any good? Even if he could knock down the wall, remove the shelves and step over there, the infected people would most likely just follow him. He remembers how Marit's dad stalked them from the other side of the windows when they were in Edith's apartment. The guy would move restlessly from side to side, following whoever was closest to him. And Hagos is convinced by now that the infected folks have gone beyond their regular, human senses such as sight and hearing. The guy on the stairs, who'd lost his eyes altogether, could not only sense them on the landing, he also found his way to the stairs with surprisingly little difficulty.

They are guided by some scary sixth sense. Some new ability that they didn't have before the infection overtook their brains.

As crazy as it sounds, Hagos doesn't consider it too far-fetched. He's watched nature programs about how pigeons and salmon and lots of other species use special imprints of the Earth's magnetic field in their nervous system to navigate across vast distances without anything to guide them except for this inherent, biological compass, driving them to breeding grounds or wherever they need to be.

What the infected people did was probably not too different. The virus—or whatever it was—clearly turned them into prey-seekers. They always know where the closest meal is—even if it's not readily accessible, they'll still be drawn to it until something else comes closer.

So, Hagos disregards the idea of reaching the other side of the closet. It would just take up a lot of effort, and probably not do him any good.

This means the only thing left is leaving the closet through the door he's currently holding shut. And that means he'll have to fight his way through the three infected people waiting right outside.

He looks at the dividing wall again. He might have to break it down anyway. Because he'll need protective layers. He would have preferred a hazmat suit or something like that, but he'll have to make do with regular clothes. If he puts enough of it on, he might just be able to push his way through the infected people and make a run for the window.

Yes, he thinks. That's my best option. That's the plan.

He kicks the dividing wall. Not terribly hard, more just like a test. His shoe breaks right through.

That was easy.

Holding the closet door with one hand, he begins tearing the hole bigger with his other hand. One at a time, the shelves are revealed. And by the time Hagos has broken down most of the wall, he realizes that he's in luck. The closet holds not only shirts, sweaters and jeans, but also heavy-duty winter boots. And from the top shelf, he pulls a basket full of gloves, scarves and even ski masks.

Perfect. This might actually work.

Hagos uses his foot to stem against the door, then begins to put on clothes.

23

As the sun sets behind the mountains, the air turns frosty. Not that the cold bothers him. He used to train up in Finnmark, where both daylight and warmth are about as rare as rocking-horse poo, so he's very much used to it.

It was actually during his stationing there that he decided to settle in Norway. People over here were just nicer compared to his native Swedes. And, more importantly, they were much more gullible. Manipulable.

Lukas was already living here, because he'd managed to knock up a blonde and wanted to be involved in the kid's life. That was typical Lukas. He was always the sentimental one. Had it been Kjell who got contacted by some broad, telling him he was going to be a dad to some kid, he'd probably have gone there to punch her hard enough in the belly to make sure she aborted. No one was going to have that kind of leverage over him. Kjell had always been a free agent—at least since he finally left home at the age of fifteen. Lukas's dad wouldn't allow him to move out until he turned eighteen. Just like Lukas had waited patiently, so would Kjell.

But Kjell grew impatient. So, he stole a clear nail polish from the woman living next door and started adding a few drops to his dad's insulin every night. It only took three weeks to do the job. One night, he heard his old man moan from his bedroom. Kjell got up, walked in there and found him on the floor, purple in the face, eyes bulging. He was going through his pants, searching for his phone. With shaking, sweating hands, he managed to pull it out, and as he was about to tap those three numbers, Kjell went over and took the phone from him.

His dad roared after him as he left the room. Kjell brought the key so he could lock the door from the outside, then simply went back to bed. He ignored the cries and the banging, and he soon drifted off.

The next morning, he woke with a feeling of elation. And as he went to his dad's bedroom, he found exactly what he'd hoped. His cold, stiff corpse.

It was deemed a heart attack. And it probably was. But no one bothered look into what had caused it. Kjell pretended to be in shock when the ambulance showed up, and the paramedics didn't suspect him of anything.

Kjell never told Lukas. But Lukas probably knew. Lukas always knew. And he always covered for him. And that was despite the fact that Lukas would never dream of doing anything like that to anyone. Lukas was always the good big brother. He never judged Kjell or ratted on him. He also never commented on any of Kjell's behavior, even when it went to the extremes—which it invariably did with frequent intervals.

Like that time in college he poked out the eye of the guy who came for him in the bathroom. As far as Kjell heard, he never saw out of that eye again. Which served him right.

Kjell always liked Lukas. He didn't love him, because love is as foreign to him as Chinese, but Lukas was the person in Kjell's life he cared most about. He had been a kind of surrogate mother for him growing up, and they still had a close relationship as adults.

Kjell always liked to have Lukas around. And as soon as it dawned on Kjell just how dangerous this current situation was, and how it's likely going to spiral out of control within weeks, turning into a global catastrophe, he went straight to Lukas. And they agreed the right cause of action was to get the hell out of Dodge. To seek refuge somewhere even more desolate. Siberia was the obvious choice for several reasons. First and foremost because of Jan's contact who would get them into Russia without anyone knowing about it. But also because both brothers were able to thrive in the harsh, cold environment.

It was a good plan. Kjell actually looked forward to it. He'd always been somewhat disenchanted with the ordinary world of men; it was just plain boring to him. So many spoken and unspoken rules. Such constraints and such a fragile foundation. He recalls watching a documentary on WWII, in which they quoted Hitler for saying about Russia, something along the lines of, "We have only to kick in the door and the whole rotten structure will come crashing down." That was how Kjell always viewed society. He knew it wasn't going to last. All it took was one hard kick.

And now, that kick had happened. And the world was crumbling. And Kjell was meant to survive in this new world. Finally, he would get to live the way he was always meant to. And his brother would be there, right beside him. Jan too, that jerky, gum-chewing moron, but only because it was his contact that would arrange the plane. After they'd reached their destination, if Jan grew too annoying, Kjell could always push him off a cliff or drown him in a lake. Lukas would turn the blind eye as he always dead.

The only problem is, that Lukas is dead. Dead as their poor old dad.

Killed by that old gnarly asshole.

Kjell is going to make him regret it. He's going to make the old guy suffer. And he's going to take his time, too. Figure out the perfect approach. He's no longer in too great of a hurry to get out of the country. Now that he's on his own, he has no one to protect, no one to answer to but himself. As sad as it is that Lukas died, there's also a great deal of freedom in his brother's death.

He reaches the highway and sits down on the guardrail. He places the rifle right next to himself and takes off his backpack. Staring out over the valley, he obviously can't see the cave—he wouldn't be able too, even in broad daylight—but he knows approximately where it is. He thinks of Lukas. His brother's body is still out there. They probably won't give him a proper burial.

Kjell notices to his surprise a pressure-like sensation in his chest. It's not unlike a chest cold, only he doesn't feel like coughing. He realizes that it's probably grief he's feeling. At least to the extent that he's able to. Kjell was always different. He knew that from early childhood. No one had to tell him so. He could tell by observing others. It always puzzled him how their faces would betray all kinds of unnecessary emotions in situations that hardly warranted it.

They would blush when they said something they regretted. They would look sad when others got hurt. They would even cry over movies.

Kjell never cried. Not even once. His eyes would run if the wind was strong or he had a nasty bout of the flu. But he'd never in his life experienced real crying.

He tries to do so now. Just as an experiment. Losing Lukas is probably the greatest loss he'll ever get to feel, so if not now, then he'll probably never cry. He's curious to find out what it's like. He leans forward, squints his eyes shut and produces the approximate sounds he's heard others make.

It doesn't work. Not a single tear.

"Oh, well," he mutters, straightening back up.

The pressure in his chest remains. But now it's morphing into something different. Something he knows very well. Anger. That's how he'll honor his brother. Not by sitting here, weeping like an old lady. But by using his rage to torture and kill the guy who shot Lukas.

He looks at the lights from the camp. How many dead people have they brought in by now? Five thousand? Even more than that? The prison, back when it was operational, could only hold five hundred prisoners, but the infected people weren't ordinary prisoners, and they didn't possess the same basic rights, so they were packed into the cells like sardines. Kjell saw it before they left. He had to have a look. The sounds were drawing him, the choir of moans echoing through the hallway. So, he peeked into the west wing, and he saw the forest of arms reaching out through the bars, and he smelled the awfulness of fever and rotting flesh. That's when he knew for a fact that the only sane thing to do was up and leave.

Kjell ponders the dilemma. There's just no way he's getting near that cave without being spotted. The old guy already had trip wires in place, and now he'll be extra careful. He's obviously no amateur, but a trained survivor. Probably ex-military. And this is his turf. He prepared that cave long before the outbreak. There's three of them, so they have every opportunity to take turns and keep watch around the clock. What Kjell needs is someone else to lead the way. Someone to go there before himself. Someone who could create the perfect distraction. Just enough to catch them off-guard.

Going back to camp and getting someone to go with him isn't viable. He knows a few of the other soldiers pretty well, but there's no way he'd be able to convince any of them to go with him on a personal vendetta, especially not one where they'd basically have to act as bait. Besides, they were all too scared to leave their duty behind. Cowards. If only—

A sound becomes audible in the silence. An engine, coming this way. It sounds bigger than a regular car. It could very well be one of the trucks from camp.

And it suddenly clicks into place. The entire plan comes to him at once. Kjell smiles in the darkness.

24

Within ten minutes, he's completely covered from top to bottom in several layers of clothes. It wasn't easy in the enclosed space of the closet, especially not since he didn't want to let go of the door for more than a split second at a time. But he managed. Besides pants and shirts, he also put on boots, gloves, even the ski mask. The only part of him not protected by fabric is his eyes.

With all the extra insulation, he's sweating profusely. His heart is also beating faster, knowing what comes next.

He moves his arms as much as he can. They have relatively fine freedom of movement. It's worse with his legs. The three pair of pants make it difficult to bend his knees more than ninety degrees.

I better not fall down, because I'm not sure I'll be able to get back up.

The thought of sliding the door open to face the three infected people makes his muscles tremble all over.

But he needs to get going. Sweat is soaking the inner layers, and he keeps having to blink it out of his eyes. If he stays in here, he'll become dehydrated within the hour.

He closes his eyes and breathes deeply. "God, let Your hand protect me, Your way lie before me, Your shield defend me. For You have armed me with strength for battle; humbled my adversaries before me. Your will be done. Amen."

Muttering the old prayer that he hasn't spoken for years, he finds the words are still right there, surprisingly fresh in memory. And they fill him with just enough courage to chase the fear away. He opens his eyes, and, before doubt can slip back into his mind and heart, he thrusts the door sideways.

He was expecting to meet the infected people right away, but he wasn't expecting them to literally fall on him. The sporty woman must have been leaning on the door, though, because she tilts forward and lands in his arms, grabbing hold of Hagos in a tight embrace. He tries to duck, but it's impossible; the woman has already wrapped her arms around his chest, pinning one of his arms, and she snaps her teeth at his face. Hagos manages to place his free hand in front of her face and save his nose at the last second. The woman isn't deterred in the least by the obstacle, she just goes to work on the glove. As she chews on three of his fingers like an eager dog with a chew toy, it feels like his fingers are being trapped in a door with someone pushing against it. But the leather holds, and it enables him to grab her jaw and force her back. Her teeth are still snapping at his fingers, but as Hagos exits the closet, he's immediately faced with bigger concerns. The two other infected guys swoop in from the sides. One grabs his arm and sinks his teeth into his shoulder. The other, who seems to have been knocked over as Hagos pushed the woman back, goes for his leg, clamping on like a playful kid.

Hagos has pushed the woman back far enough that the embrace is broken, and his other arm is free again. In his hand is the belt, and he already formed it into a noose. Now, he slips it over the head of the guy working on his leg, and as he pulls it hard, the noose tightens around his neck, effectively turning him into a dog on a leash. But he's still holding onto Hagos's leg, making it difficult to turn, so he has no choice but to press on forward. He uses all his strength to force the woman backwards, while dragging along both of the guys. All four of them move like a single unit, with Hagos doing all the work, and he's already heaving for breath. The world is fiery hot, hands are grabbing him all over, teeth gnawing away at him, grunts and snarls filling his ears.

Reaching the bed, he forces the woman down on it, then, still holding her jaw, he twists her head hard to the side, hoping to get her to stop biting so he can get his hand free. He puts way too much force behind the movement, though, and he feels her jaw pop as it's dislocated. Which achieves the result he was hoping for: The woman is no longer able to close her mouth, and Hagos can finally retract his hand. The glove is all chewed up and wet from foamy saliva, but it's still clinging on, and it doesn't appear to have been torn open.

Staggering backwards, he wants to get away from the woman before she can get back up and grab him again. But the guys are really going at it from both sides, and Hagos only manages a couple of steps, almost losing his balance. He yanks the belt, trying to strangle the guy on the left, while swatting at the other guy. But the glove on his hand now serves as an unhandy cushion, softening the blows. Even as Hagos lands a couple of wild swings on the sides of the guy's head, he's barely rocked by it.

Instead, Hagos tries to rip free, thrusting to the left, dragging along the guy on the leash. But the other guy is too strong, and he manages to hold on. And now the woman is coming back, her open mouth grinning crookedly at him. Hagos tries in desperation to yank the guy on the leash in front of him, using him as a shield against the woman, but his strength is failing him now, his body is exhausted, and the woman shoves aside the guy to grab Hagos by the collar and lean in for another bite.

Had her jaw been working, she would have no doubt dug her teeth into his face. Instead, all she manages is to breathe and slobber all over his chin and mouth, like a drunk girl eager to French kiss him. Hagos cries out and tries to veer back, but he's pinned in place by the guys, and his only option is to fling the woman a vicious headbutt.

His forehead connects with the bridge of her nose, audibly breaking it, and she reels back, but doesn't let go of him.

Hagos turns his head this way then that. The world is awfully narrow, appearing to him through a cloudy veil, and he sees the open window, then the open door, and since the door is closer, he makes a snap decision and goes for it.

He has no strength left. He can barely move his legs. He doesn't worry about fighting the infected people anymore. He just moves for the door as fast as he can—which isn't very fast at all. They're all clinging to him like wasps on a rotten apple. Hagos focuses completely on the doorway, blocking out everything else. He lifts one leg, moves it forward, puts it back down, then moves the other. Slowly, slowly, he gets closer to the door. The infected people aren't letting go. And he's not moving fast enough to shake them.

If I can just make it to the stairs. I'll throw myself down the steps.

It's insane. But it's his last hope.

He reaches the doorway, grabs hold of the frame with his hand, seeing to his horror that the glove is now hanging in tatters, exposing his fingers. He pulls himself forward with one last burst of effort, roaring out as he does.

The movement causes the woman to trip and fall down. Hagos stumbles over her and falls too. Landing on his stomach, he tries briefly to get back up, but soon realizes it's no use. The infected are crawling on him, weighing him down, tearing, chewing their way through the layers of clothes.

Hagos instead claws his way forward. The tile floor is awfully smooth, and he actually manages to move forward. Hagos moves his arms, blocking out everything else. The staircase is twelve feet away. Ten. Six.

He's very close. Almost within reach.

And then the woman suddenly comes crawling over his head, blocks his view as she sits down on his shoulders and begins tearing at the top of his head, clearly wanting to pull the ski mask off, exposing his skull. And she almost manages. Hagos grabs hold of it at the last moment, yanking it back down. But the eye holes have moved an inch up, and he can no longer see anything but darkness.

This is it, he realizes, as he's forced to stop moving forward. Instead, he pulls his arms and legs in as much as he can, while still clinging on to the ski mask. *Please, God. Let it be fast.*

His thoughts go to Abeba. He tries to take solace in the fact that he'll get to see her again soon.

Then, as the infected people rip and tear away at him, he begins praying.

25

"You bought it, Sarge?"

Gorm blinks and looks at Nils, who's driving the truck, his bloodshot eyes fixed on the dark road ahead. Gorm himself was almost drifting off. Ove is sleeping next to him, snoring loudly, leaning against the door. He doesn't blame the guy; they're all going on forty hours without sleep now. As soon as they bring this round of infected people back, they're gonna sleep. Gorm doesn't give a damn if there's no one else to cover for them; as dire as the situation is, they can't be expected to go for days without sleep.

"Bought what?" Gorm asks, clearing his throat.

"Her story." Nils tilts his head back, gesturing towards the passengers. "About the mono?"

"Oh." Gorm hadn't given it much thought. To him, the woman was just another SI they couldn't allow to go free. Of course, it wasn't fun taking her away from her daughter—Gorm has two kids of his own, a few years older than the girl, but still only kids, so he can only imagine how hard it must be for the woman. "Yeah, I think there's a fair chance she might be telling the truth. Of course, she had plenty of reason to lie, but you never know, do you?"

"Her wound," Nils goes on. "I just don't think it looked like a scratch mark. Struck me more like a rope burn."

"Could be."

Gorm reaches for the air-freshener mounted on the dashboard. He gives it a squeeze, but no vapor comes out.

"It ran out an hour ago," Nils remarks.

Gorm leans back with a grunt. The smell from the back of the truck is noticeable even up here, even with the heater blowing at high, and they can't really roll down the windows.

Gorm leans back his head, hoping Nils will drop the subject. His thoughts go to Louise and the kids. As soon as he gets the chance, he'll call them. Let them know he's all right, that he's keeping out of danger. Which isn't totally true, but—

"What are we doing here, Sarge?" Gorm opens his eyes to see Nils staring at him. His eyes aren't just bloodshot—they're glassy, beyond tired, scared shitless. "Stock-piling infected people? And bringing along some folks who don't even have the virus? I mean, what's the point?"

Gorm takes a deep breath through his nose. "You're tired, Nils. Don't indulge in such existential thoughts when you're this played out. It won't do any good."

Nils looks back out onto the road, shaking his head. "It's like with the death penalty and why it's wrong."

"How so?"

Nils shrugs. "Let's say some people truly deserve to die. Some straight-up sociopaths who can't be redeemed and will never stop killing. Sure, they deserve the needle. But others don't. They're just messed up. Was in the wrong place at the wrong time. They could be helped. The problem is, we can't tell the difference. And even if we could, who the hell are we to decide who lives and dies? Are we gods?"

Gorm grunts. "Last time I checked, there was nothing divine about me, that's for sure."

"Exactly," Nils says, not smiling.

"So, what's your point exactly?"

"Some of those people we've brought back, they shouldn't have come. But we took them anyway. Like the woman. I don't think she's infected. But we hauled her along, and now she'll probably catch the virus, and her poor daughter will never see her again." He's breathing fast now. "My point is, since we can't tell for sure who deserves to die, we shouldn't execute anyone."

"Okay," Gorm says, considering it. "So, you'd have us let all SIs go free? What about those who really are infected? Those who are lying, or who don't even know they're infected? What about the people they'll go on to infect once they turn? Won't those lives be on us as well?"

Nils falls silent.

"This isn't a perfect solution," Gorm goes on, "but it's the best we can do for now. Isolate them until we know for sure."

"But that's just the thing," Nils says, looking over at him again. "The tests aren't conclusive. They can't diagnose this virus—if that's what it is."

Gorm frowns. "How do you know?"

"I spoke with Leila, you know, one of the physicians they brought in? The one with the—"

"Yeah, yeah, she's got that birthmark."

"Exactly. She told me they can only tell if the person's ... what was it? ... some kinda numbers are elevated, I don't remember what she called it. But she said it might as well be from a common cold. They just don't know. How many people do you think's got the sniffles this time of year, Sarge? Basically everyone."

"So, we keep them isolated until we do know for sure," Gorm says. "That seems only reasonable to me."

Nils scoffs. "Yeah, 'isolated.' You know they're putting them in with the others, right?"

"Of course they don't. They get their own cells."

"That's what I mean. The false positives are locked in with the true positives. You don't see a problem with that?"

Gorm turns in the seat to face Nils. "Okay, look, you either shut the hell up, or you tell me what you'd have us do. Should we pull over right here? Kick the woman off? Tell her, 'sorry, good luck'?"

Nils doesn't answer right away. Just as he seems about to, his eyes widen. "Look, Sarge."

Gorm follows his gaze. A figure is coming into view. The uniform is immediately recognizable. The soldier is standing in the middle of the road, waving with both arms.

"Holy shit," Gorm mutters as Nils slows down. "Is that ... Hedlund?"

"Who?"

"Hedlund, Sarge. The Swede?"

"Oh, him. Damnit, I think you're right. Stop the truck, Nils."

26

They've been driving for half an hour.

The mood in the car is heavy to say the least. No one is talking.

Aksel's eyelids are getting heavy, too. He's constantly blinking, trying to stay awake.

A light snow has begun to drizzle. It's that powdery, crispy stuff that you'll only see when there's absolutely no wind. The crystals are so thin, they almost seem able to stay afloat in the air. Aksel never gave a damn about the different types of snow, but living in the northern part of Norway, it's second nature to him. He knows this is likely the onslaught of a heavy downpour. It could come before dawn, or it could hold off for another couple of days. But he's ninety percent sure a lot more snow is to come.

"If we're really unlucky, the roads will become impassable," Anne mutters, as though reading his mind. "I mean, it's not like they'll be worrying about clearing them."

"I know," Aksel says, stretching. "We'll just have to hope."

Anne turns on the wipers, and they effortlessly push aside the snowflakes that melt the moment they touch the windscreen.

Aksel notices two tire tracks appearing on the now-white road. "Huh. Looks like we're on the right path."

Anne suddenly stomps the brake, almost causing the MPV to go skidding. They come to a halt in the middle of the road, and she kills the light.

"Why are we stopping?" Rosa asks from the back.

"What are you seeing?" Aksel asks, looking from Anne to the whiteness outside. She's staring ahead, squinting.

"Taillights," she says, putting the MPV in reverse. "They've stopped."

As Anne begins backing up, turning in her seat to see the road, Aksel finally makes out two small red lights a few hundred yards ahead. He's impressed that Anne even picked up on them. Her eyes must be excellent.

"Why have they stopped?" Rosa asks.

"Probably to pick up more infected people," Folmer mutters.

"That, or they could have run into trouble," Aksel says.

"What kind of trouble?" Rosa asks, concern in her voice.

"I don't know," he says, sending her an earnest look. "Perhaps they slid off the road, or the engine died. Who knows?"

Anne backs up a little more, until they're out of sight behind the curve in the road. She stops the car and looks ahead. "I say we wait here. Check in another five minutes if they've kept going."

Aksel bites his lip. "Or maybe this is our chance."

"How so?" Anne asks, sending him a sideways glance. "I hope you're not suggesting we bum-rush them."

"No, that'd be suicide. But I could sneak up there. Try and get Belinda out. If they're busy loading more infected people on the truck, they might not see me. Or, better yet, if they're bogged down for some reason, they're probably staying in the cockpit to keep warm."

"That still sounds risky to me," Anne says.

"I'll be the only one running the risk. You guys stay here, stay out of sight. And even if they spot me, I really don't think they'll shoot me. Worst case scenario, they'll bring me along. If I'm not back in five minutes, you'll have to assume that's what happened." He's unbuckling as he speaks. "And if so, then just follow the original plan. Follow them to the camp and figure out a way to get in."

"You're really doing this?" Anne asks.

Aksel nods, pulling up his hoodie and tying in the strings. "I'm sure it'll be a lot easier breaking her out of a truck than out of a prison."

"At least bring the dog, then."

Aksel glances back at Guardian. The dog is looking at him, seemingly ready and willing to go with him.

"No," Aksel decides. "I need to move quickly and quietly."

The real reason is that he figures there's a real risk of the soldiers shooting the dog if they see it and consider it a threat.

"Okay," he says, opening the door. Immediately, the icy air and the frozen snowflakes whirl inside the car. He glances back at Anne one last time. "Five minutes. Then consider me gone."

She nods.

"Be careful, Aksel," Rosa tells him.

"I will," he says.

Then he steps out and closes the door as quietly as he can. Bowing his head, he begins jogging down the powdered road, breathing in the freezing air, squinting against the falling snow.

27

First order of business is getting out of here.

Then, she needs to find a charger. Get her phone back on. Call her mom, tell her the good news.

Ella still isn't exactly sure if this really is good news. She assumes so. Having survived the infection, and now, apparently being nonexistent in the eyes of the undead, that's got to be cause for celebration.

Yet she can't help but feel a bit … unreal. Almost like she's not really here anymore. Maybe it's just her mind that's fighting to catch up. She was absolutely set on dying. She'd come to terms with it. She was ready. She even said her goodbyes.

And now, she finds herself still alive. She got a second chance. She should be ecstatic. But right now, all she feels is confusion and—oddly enough—a mild amusement. For some reason, the situation is almost funny to her. Having prepared herself to die, saying goodbye to her mother … and then not dying after all. There's something comical about it. Like a balloon growing to the point of explosion, then instead the air just seeps out with an anticlimactic whiz.

Real or not, she still wants to call her mom.

So, she goes to the window. The undead couple are both pressing against the glass, making half-hearted attempts at getting out. As there is no live prey out there, the zombies seem almost lazy. Like they're saving energy. It's very different from how she's seen them act with determination whenever they're close to someone to attack.

"Excuse me," she says, almost bursting into laughter. "Could you move aside, please?"

The guy is blocking the terrace door, but he doesn't react to Ella's voice.

So, she reaches out a hand, places it on his shoulder, and pushes him gently sideways. He takes a few staggering steps, gives a grunt, but doesn't bother looking at her.

They really don't care. They don't even sense me. I'm like a piece of furniture to them.

"Couch coming through," she says, and this time she can't help but snicker. The situation is simply too surreal.

She opens the terrace door and steps outside. As she tries to close it behind her, the woman steps in from the other side.

"Sorry," Ella says, instinctively placing a hand on her collarbone to hold her back. "You're staying here."

She closes the door in the face of the woman, and she begins fumbling over the glass, her black eyes looking right through Ella.

Immediately, the icy air fills her lungs and filters out the awful stench of blood and death. She takes a couple of deep breaths.

Okay, where am I going?

The answer is simple, really. She needs her charger, and that's still back at Gunnar and Greta's place. She could press through the trees, but it's probably easier just walking around to the front end of the nursing home. So she does. As she reaches the parking lot, she sees three police cars parked haphazardly. All of them empty. The glass doors of the nursing home have been shot or smashed open, and the entrance hall is empty too—anyone infected has probably left the building to go find fresh meat. The cops are nowhere to be seen. Ella is willing to bet they're all either zombies by now, or perhaps some of them had the wit to run the hell away. She certainly wouldn't blame any officers of the law for abandoning their duty in a situation like this.

As Ella crosses the parking lot, she suddenly catches a movement from the side. The patrol cars aren't empty after all. Inside the nearest is a head, peering out at her. It's a man, not much older than Ella, and he apparently sought refuge in the police car.

Ella stops and looks back at him. "It's okay," she says. "You can come out. I don't think there is anyone infected left."

The guy just stares at her, not saying anything.

Ella steps a little closer. "Look, you can wait for help if you want, but I'm not sure anyone is coming by anytime soon. I think it's more likely someone infected will show up and trap you in there."

"Get away!" the guy shrieks, raising his hand to point a handgun at Ella. "Get away from me!"

Ella stops abruptly. Her first thought is that the cops left a gun lying in the car, and the guy found it and picked it up. But as he raises his hand, his sleeve and collar come into view, and Ella recognizes the jacket—it's exactly like her mother's.

He's a cop, Ella realizes to her astonishment. The guy can't be more than twenty-two. Probably fresh out of the academy. They probably didn't teach the poor guy to deal with dead people trying to eat everyone.

Ella backs away as she holds up her hands.

"You're not getting in here," the young cop tells her, his voice breaking. "I'll shoot you if you try."

"It's fine, I don't want to get in the car," Ella assures him. "But you should really drive away while you have the chance."

The cop blinks. "I don't ... I don't have the keys."

"Oh. Then maybe get out and run."

He shakes his head firmly. "I'm not going out there." He doesn't need to elaborate; it's all in his eyes. What he's seen. What happened to all his colleagues. "Get the hell away from here, okay? Before you draw any of them to me."

"Sure," Ella says, not bothering to explain anything. "Best of luck."

The guy just blinks.

Ella goes to the sidewalk and heads for her aunt and uncle's house. The street looks like she expected. Corpses, bullets, more vehicles left or crashed. A growl from the opposite side of the street makes her turn her head. A kid is busy eating away at someone else. Ella can't tell if it's a guy or a girl, because the face is covered in blood. But as the kid apparently loses interest in the meal and stands up on wobbly legs, she can tell they're very young. Middle-grade. They're wearing a Harry Potter shirt.

"Jesus," she whispers.

The kid glances briefly in her direction, then heads instead for the parking lot she just left.

Within a few seconds, the person on the ground sits up with a jolt. It's a woman—could be the kid's mom, or could be someone unrelated. She looks after the child, giving of a groan, as though asking, "Hey, are we done here?" Then she gets to her feet, which isn't easy, because as she does, most of her intestines plop out onto the pavement. She doesn't seem bothered by it; she just walks right over them, almost tripping, as she follows the kid down the street.

Ella swallows hard. She considers briefly going back to the cop car and offer him to push the cadavers aside so he can get out. He must see them coming, because they're heading right for his car. But she knows the young cop won't take her offer. He'll burrow down and stay in the car, and he'll likely either die of thirst or finally get desperate enough to make a run for it. Hopefully, by then, he won't be too weak to make it.

But, as Ella turns away, the cop makes a different decision.

A gunshot rings out, and Ella turns back around, covering her ears, expecting more bullets to fly. She's expecting to see the car door or maybe the window open, the cop aiming the gun at the oncoming infected people.

Instead, she sees nothing. None of the car's doors are open, nor the windows. The kid and the woman were almost there, but now, to Ella's surprise, they stop. Standing there for a moment, it's almost like they reconsider the situation. Then they get moving again. But they no longer go for the cop car. Instead, they head to the nearest driveway and disappears from sight.

Ella frowns, looking back at the car, wondering what just happened.

Then it hits home, and her stomach drops.

She doesn't even need to go back there to check if she's right. The zombies sudden loss of interest tells her all she needs to know.

They no longer cared about the cop car because there was no one alive inside it anymore.

28

She's fighting against the panic that's gnawing away right below her chest bone. It feels like a desperate rat is trapped in there, thrashing, trying to claw its way out.

I need to stay strong. For Rosa's sake.

Surprisingly, thinking of her daughter doesn't make the panic worse. In fact, it seems to lower it somewhat.

I'll get to see her again. One way or the other.

She forces herself to breathe through her nose, even though the smell in here is absolutely rancid. But inhaling through her mouth not only goes against what her yoga teacher told her about calming the nervous system—it also hurts like hell in her throat. Compared to the panic rat in her chest, the red-hot lump of molten lava at the back of her tongue is much more painful. Every time she swallows, it feels like a cactus is being forced down her esophagus. The mono has never been this bad before.

She has no idea how long they've been driving. Her sense of time is probably unreliable, but at least she can tell it's still dark outside. She knows because it's dark in here, too. Pitch black, in fact. She can only make out vague outlines of her fellow passengers. But she can hear them.

At first, the choir of moans and groans, the snapping of teeth, and the bumps from skulls bouncing off the walls were causing her panic to go through the roof. Now, she's a little more able to ignore it. Or, at least not feel terrified by it. As awful as the zombies sound—kinda like animals, but not quite; it's more like someone in agony, someone longing for relief but unable to do anything about it—she's at least convinced by now that they can't get to her. That the straps will hold.

Still, all it takes is one of the leather strops to break. If one of the infected should get free, they will no doubt head right for her, and she will be completely defenseless. Strapped to her seat, unable to move her head more than a little bit, she has nothing to ward off an attacker, and she will get eaten alive.

She tries very hard not to think of it. It makes the panic rat go crazy.

The old guy in the hunting coat next to her was completely quiet for the first five minutes or so. Then he suddenly began moving and snarling, and Belinda knew she was the only one still alive in the back of the truck. And now she's—

The truck suddenly slows down, cutting her train of thought.

The driver doesn't ease off the gas like you'd do when coming up on a bend or somewhere you need to make a turn. He does it abruptly, like when you suddenly see an obstacle on the road.

Oh, God. They've probably stopped more infected people.

Seeming to confirm her suspicion, the truck comes to a full stop. Ignoring the sounds from the zombies as best she can, she hears the soldiers up front exchange words. She can't make out what they're saying, but judging from their voices, they sound surprised. It sounds like one of the doors open, and then the sergeant calls out: "Hey, Kjell. Didn't expect to see you out here ..."

More words Belinda can't make out. Apparently, they're talking to someone out there.

Then, out of nowhere, three rapid gunshots very close by. Belinda jolts, banging her head against the wall.

The sound of running footsteps.

One of the soldiers shouts: "*What are you doing? **No, no, no!***"

Then two more shots, and finally, silence.

Belinda breathes fast, listening intently, trying hard to figure out what she just heard.

Someone shot someone, that much is she certain of. But who, and why? Whomever the soldiers stopped for, they obviously knew them.

Her first thought was that the soldiers must have opened fire on someone infected who somehow surprised them and got too close. But there were no warning calls. No one giving their friends a heads-up before opening fire.

And the silence she's hearing now is very puzzling, too. If anyone is still alive out there, why aren't they talking?

Suddenly, the lock on the door at the back of the truck is turned and one of the doors pulled open.

Belinda leans forward to see a faint glow coming in. A dark figure is standing in the opening. She's about to call out, but something holds her back. Then the person turns on a bright flashlight. The sudden light blinds. She blinks and pulls her head back. The person by the door pans the light around for a few moments. Then he calls out: "Anyone alive in here?"

Belinda doesn't answer. She can tell it's not one of the soldiers who picked her up, and she suddenly feels pretty sure the person out there shot all three of them.

Finally, he mutters something, then closes the door again.

Belinda lets out a long, trembling breath through the muzzle.

A couple of minutes pass. She can't really hear anything, so she has no idea what's going on outside. The truck's engine just keeps idling.

Suddenly, the lock is turned once more, and the door opens again.

Belinda's heart ups its speed. She leans back her head and squeezes her eyes shut. She's sure that this time, the guy will make a more thorough inspection of the truck, and he will notice that she's still alive, and he will very likely kill her on the spot, just like he did with the others.

"Belinda?"

She blinks her eyes open. Hearing her name is such a surprise, she doesn't immediately react.

"*Belinda?*" the person by the door asks again. "You still in here?"

This time, she recognizes the voice.

29

She's just about to turn into the driveway of Gunnar and Greta's, when she hears an engine roar to life.

From the next house over comes a car bolting out of the driveway. It's going way too fast, and the driver seems to realize, because they hit the brakes hard, causing the car to stop just a few feet before it would have plowed through the hedge of the garden of the adjacent house. The engine dies, but instead the wipers begin going—even though there's no sign of rain.

Ella squints to try and make out who's behind the wheel. Judging by the reckless driving, it's either someone without a license, or someone who's seriously ill. She can't make out the driver because of how the pale sunlight is hitting the windscreen.

The engine comes back to life, the wipers stop, and the car lurches forward, tires screeching. Ella moves to the side, wanting to be sure the car won't hit her. It swerves a little, but doesn't come too close. As it passes her, though, she catches glimpse of the driver—and she exclaims: "Marit?"

Her cousin sees her and locks the brakes once more—this time, she manages to keep the engine going. She just sits there, staring at Ella for several seconds, her expression a mixture of confusion, trepidation and disbelief.

Ella goes towards the car, smiling. "Hi, Marit. I'm glad to see you're still OK."

Marit moves her mouth, but she doesn't appear to be actually saying anything. She shakes her head and blinks several times.

"I know," Ella says. "I'm as surprised as you, believe me."

Marit says something Ella can't make out.

Ella tries to open the door, but Marit scrambles to slam down the lock before she can do it.

Ella can't help but laugh. "Listen, it's all right. I'm not a zombie. I hope you can tell." She runs her hands up and down her own sides, as though displaying a wonderful dress. "In fact, I feel perfectly fine."

Marit says a single word. It looks like "how?"

"Could you roll down the window at least?" Ella asks.

Marit fumbles for the button, clearly not wanting to take her eyes off of Ella. She rolls the window down half an inch, but leaves her finger on the button.

"How are you ... not dead?"

"Beats me," Ella says earnestly, adding in her mind: *And yeah, I'm glad to see me alive too, Marit.* Out loud, she says: "I somehow kicked the infection. And as a bonus, the zombies don't care about me anymore. I've gained some kind of immunity."

Marit doesn't look any less suspicious at this. "Are you sure?"

"I'm still not sure of anything, tell you the truth," Ella admits. "But for each minute that passes, it feels more and more real. Hey, where's Hagos?"

Marit's eyes flicker. "Hagos? He didn't make it."

"Oh. That's too bad."

"Yeah." Marit chews her lip. "Are you sure it's not just that ... it hasn't killed you yet?"

"I'm fairly sure, yeah. The fever broke. I'm not even sick anymore. Look." She pulls up her sleeve to slow the scratches. The swelling has gone down, and while they're still bright pink, they look a lot more like regular scratches. Like something from a branch or a disgruntled kitty.

"I don't ... I don't believe it," Marit says.

"Yeah, me neither," Ella smiles. "So, look, can I just get my charger, and we can get going?"

"No," Marit says, shaking her head. "No, I mean, I don't believe that you're not sick. They said it so many times on television ... no one beat it. Every single one who caught it ended up as those nasty things. It had a hundred percent molarity rate."

"Mortality," Ella corrects her, shrugging. "And I guess I'm the first one, then."

Marit eyes her. "But my dad, he got it, and it ... it killed him." Her voice becomes thinner. "Why would he die from it and not you? He was a lot stronger than you."

Maybe he wasn't as strong as you thought, Ella thinks, feeling her anger towards Marit intensify. She reminds herself that her cousin just lost both her parents, and she's likely in shock. "Look, I can't explain it," Ella says. "Right now, I just need to get the charger for my phone so I can call my mom, and then we'll get as far away from here as possible. Hey, wait, do you have your phone? You have her number, right?"

"I do," Marit says, sounding thoughtful.

"Can I please borrow it? It'll just be a sec. You don't have to let me inside the car if you're still not comfortable. Just, please, let me call my mom and tell her I'm alive."

Marit breathes through her nose. "I don't think that's a good idea, Ella."

"Why not?"

Ella almost shouts, and she regrets it immediately, because Marit jolts, then promptly rolls up the window. She fumbles with the gearshift.

"Oh, come on, Marit," Ella says, stepping over to tap the window. "I'm telling you, I'm fine!"

Marit leans away from the window, revving up the engine, but the car doesn't move, because she hasn't managed to put it in Drive.

Ella moves to the front of the car and looks at her cousin through the windscreen. "Please, Marit. This is silly. I promise, I won't touch you. Let's forget about the charger and just get out of here."

"Move aside!" Marit says, waving at her. "I'm going now, Ella. I don't want to run you over, but I will if you force me!"

To prove her point, she steps on the gas, making the engine roar. Ella shrugs. "Okay, fine. I just figured we'd have a better chance of making it out of here together. But if you don't trust me, then—"

"Watch out!" Marit suddenly shouts, pointing across the street.

Ella looks in the direction. She didn't hear the guy coming, probably because Marit is busy revving it up. He looks relatively unscathed, save for a bruised shin, which is visible because he's only wearing a bathrobe. Luckily, it's still tied together at the waist, because judging by his chest, he appears to be naked underneath.

Marit is shouting something from inside the car.

Ella stays in place, watching the guy carefully. As she expected, he looks right past her and in at Marit. He comes very close, but he doesn't even try to attack Ella. Instead, he staggers around her, then goes to work on the window next to Marit. Marit stares from the guy to Ella.

"See?" Ella says, throwing out her arms. "I'm not interesting to them anymore."

Marit swallows visibly. "That ... that doesn't prove anything. That just means the infection is still in your blood."

Ella realizes to her annoyance that there's no way she can convince Marit. The worst part about it is that she understands her cousin's skepticism. No one knows what this is or how it behaves. All anyone knows is that it's extremely dangerous and contagious. If Marit could feel what Ella is feeling—that she's not sick anymore, that she's kicked the infection completely—she might have believed her. But, looking from Marit's perspective, it only makes sense not to take any chances.

"I'm sorry to leave you like this," Marit goes on—trying hard to ignore the zombie and focus on Ella. "I really am. But I'm going now."

"Good luck," Ella says, moving aside.

As Marit gets the car moving, she suddenly seems to recall something, and she stops to look at Ella again. "By the way … I wouldn't go back for the charger if I was you."

Ella frowns. "Why not?"

"I just wouldn't go in that house." Marit sends her an earnest look which Ella can't really discern. But she knows her well enough to tell there's something she doesn't want to spill. "Bye, Ella."

Ella watches as Marit drives off. The zombie tries to follow along for a few yards, but is quickly left behind. He grunts with disappointment, then turns to face Ella.

"Sorry," Ella tells him. "I tried to make her stay."

The guy snaps his jaws a couple of times, then shambles off in a seemingly random direction.

Ella turns towards Gunnar and Greta's house. She's not sure what Marit's warning was supposed to mean. Whatever is in there, it could be something dangerous. But the infected aren't a threat to Ella anymore. And besides, why didn't Marit just state it outright if that was what she was referring to?

No, there was something in there Marit didn't want Ella to see. Not because it could hurt Ella, but … why, then? What was it Ella had seen in Marit's face just now? Shame? Guilt, even?

Even as she's still pondering the question, she finds herself moving towards the driveway. Looking up at the house, she sees the front door open wide. And around the corner, from the garden, comes a heavy woman dressed in even heavier clothes—like she was about to go skiing when she was attacked and killed. As she rounds the corner and staggers into the house, Ella sees a huge crater in her pants, revealing that most of her left thigh and buttocks are gone.

Someone's in there, Ella realizes. *Someone who's still alive.*

Through her mind flashes Marit's face as she says, "*Hagos? He didn't make it.*"

Ella gasps, then runs into the house.

30

He didn't plan on killing those three guys. He really didn't.

After all, they didn't really deserve it. They'd done nothing to wrong him in any way. They weren't even a threat; he could tell they were buying his BS story, so he could have simply gone along with them, and they'd have taken him back to camp without any raised eyebrows. Because even if they were suspicious of him—which the Sarge probably was—they wouldn't want to accuse him of anything. They were all soldiers. Brothers in arms. They didn't rat on each other. Especially not in times like these.

Which made killing them all the more despicable. Kjell was very much aware of that. He just couldn't help it. The moment he saw them, he realized how easy it would be. They were out here all alone, miles away from any other living person. No one would ever know. The three soldiers were like pieces of free candy, just waiting for Kjell to pick them up and put them in his mouth. Guilty pleasures.

And so he shot them, and it felt amazing.

Staring down at the corpses in front of him, he can barely see straight, so fast is his pulse going behind his eyes. His throat is all tight, too, and so is his penis. It always happens. Whenever he performs any kind of violence, his member becomes rock-hard and presses against the inside of his pants, as though wanting to jump out and join the action. The strange thing about it is that Kjell isn't a homosexual, and certainly not a necrophile. But, having experienced these involuntary, bloodshed-induced raging hard-ons ever since puberty, he hardly pays the saluting Mini-Kjell any notice. Instead, he just puts his gun back in the holster and begins clearing the road.

Dragging the bodies off to the side, he hoists them up over the guardrail and shoves them out over the hillside. They go tumbling down, crashing through the bushes, disappearing from sight. Even if a police car passed by here, they wouldn't notice anything. By dawn, there'd be little left of the soldiers. Predators would see to that. He's pretty certain the infected aren't drawn to dead meat, but lynxes, wolves, foxes, even bears and eagles were native to these parts of the country, and—

Kjell freezes on his way back to the truck.

He only needs to get Nils out. The guy is hanging from the seat belt. But a movement from the rear caught his eye, and he automatically pulls out his gun again.

Whoever—or whatever—he saw, has now pulled in behind the truck. Because his mind was preoccupied with predators, his first thought is that it could have been an animal. Except it was too tall for that—short of a brown bear on its hind legs, or a fucking moose, no wild animals stand at six feet.

It was a person.

Somehow, he knows.

Someone was watching him, and they pulled back the moment he turned around.

It couldn't have been a zombie. They wouldn't be hiding like that. And it also couldn't have been someone from inside the truck. Because the rear doors can only be opened from the outside—Kjell made sure of that.

Must have been a passerby then. A curious cat who came this way and spotted the truck. Except he didn't hear an engine. And there are no other vehicles behind the truck.

Kjell crouches down and looks under the truck. Nothing to see.

He gets back up and moves slowly around to the back of the truck, eyes and ears ready, gun in his hand, ready to fire at anything that moves.

31

Coming up on the truck, Aksel moves along the shoulder of the road, keeps his head low and runs as fast as he can on the snowy ground.

He reaches the back and stops to listen for a second. He can hear the zombies inside groan, thumping against the wall. They all sound like they're still strapped in.

He peers around the corner to the front of the truck. And what he sees isn't exactly encouraging.

The passenger side door is open, and from it hangs one of the soldiers, head down. He's caught in the seatbelt, which he seems to have unbuckled just before he died. He's not a zombie—and it's not a zombie that killed him, either. That much is evident from the bullet wound in his temple, which has oozed a fair amount of blood into the snow.

What the hell? Did they suddenly decide to kill each other?

Perhaps one of them was infected, and the others found out. Still, it seems unlikely the soldiers would simply execute their colleague on the spot like that, not even bothering to haul him properly out of the truck first. Maybe a scuffle broke out between them, or maybe—

A movement from farther away catches his eye.

Someone—another soldier, judging by the uniform—is dragging another guy towards the guardrail. With a grunt, he hoists him up, tilts him over, and gives him a shove that's hard enough to send him rolling down the hillside. As he turns around, Aksel pulls his head back. He kneels down and looks under the truck. He sees the soldier's leg as he comes back and begins freeing the soldier hanging from the seat belt. The corpse slumps to the ground, and the soldier drags him the same way as the other.

Aksel has no idea what's happening. For now, he welcomes it as an opportunity to free Belinda. So, he unlocks the truck door and opens it as quietly as he can. His eyes are already tuned into the darkness, or he wouldn't have been able to see the rows of dead people staring out at him.

"Belinda?" he whispers, stepping up into the truck. "*Belinda*? You still in here?"

He recalls where she was sitting—on the left, all the way back—and he tries hard to make her out behind the others.

The shadow of her head comes into view as she leans forward as much as the straps allow her. "Aksel?" Her voice is barely more than a whimper.

"Yeah, it's me," he says, moving down the middle of the truck—making sure to keep his hands close to his body. The truck is wide enough that the zombies can't reach him, even if they stretch out their legs. But he doesn't want to take any chances. Reaching Belinda, she grabs his shirt like a drowning person and pulls him tight.

"Thank you, thank you," she whispers hoarsely. "Thank you for coming back, Aksel."

"Don't mention it," he says in her ear, prying her hands free as gently as he can. "Let me get those straps off you. We need to get the hell out of here."

"He killed them," Belinda whispers, staring at him with wide eyes. "They stopped to pick him up, and he—"

"Yeah, I know," Aksel cuts her off, placing a finger over his lips. "Keep quiet, or he'll hear us." He fumbles with the strap buckle. "Fuck, how does this thing work?"

He manages to get it open, and Belinda immediately gets to her feet.

As she does, Aksel turns towards the back of the truck, and he sees the silhouette of the guy step into view.

Quickly, he shoves Belinda back down, then takes a seat next to her. Sending her a sideways glance, he shushes without making a sound, hoping she can make out the gesture in the darkness.

Apparently, she can—or maybe she just saw the guy by the door—because she stays completely still and quiet.

A beam of light cuts through the darkness.

"Hey, asshole!" the soldier calls out. "Come say hello."

Aksel holds his breath.

"Not interested in talking? Well, I see your footprints in the snow, and there are no prints leading back again, so I know you're in here. Can't imagine why you'd hitch a ride, but suit yourself. I need someone living, and I guess you just volunteered."

With that, he slams the door and turns the lock.

"Fuck," Aksel mutters. "Who the hell is that guy?"

Belinda breathes in the darkness. "I have no idea ... like I said, they stopped to pick him up, and he just ... started shooting."

Aksel hears the driver's side door slam shut, and a moment later, the truck gets moving again.

"Where do you think he's taking us?" Aksel asks. "Did he say anything?"

"No, nothing," Belinda whispers, shaking her head. "Your guess is as good as mine."

Aksel bites his lip. "Well, I think it's safe to say he's not taking us to the quarantine zone ..."

***

Want to read Halgrim's notes and find out what happened to him and his wife?

Get the **free** prequel, *Draug*, now.

Only available at
nick-clausen.com/draug

Or, continue to book 5:
nick-clausen.com/cadaver5

Printed in Great Britain
by Amazon